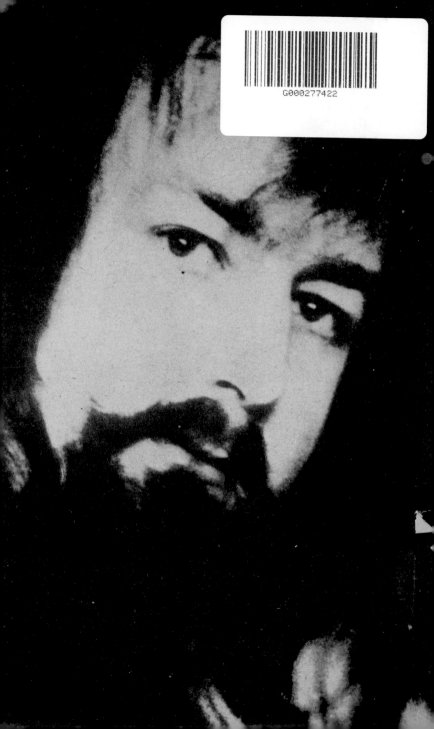

Published by Savoy Books Ltd., Manchester

ISBN 0 7045 0241 0

Printed in Great Britain by The Anchor Press Ltd
Tiptree, Essex

SOJAN

Michael Moorcock

SAVOY

INTRODUCTION

In 1957 Michael Moorcock held the editorship of TARZAN ADVENTURES, a weekly magazine published by Westworld Publications. TARZAN ADVENTURES was devoted to the characters created by Edgar Rice Burroughs and also helped introduce many related, often esoteric fantasy authors to a general readership.

In this specially prepared edition of Moorcockiana we have gathered together the juvenile fantasy stories penned by Michael Moorcock and published in TARZAN ADVENTURES under his editorial reign. In addition we have selected a number of other rarely printed and unpublished works from a variety of sources and periods. They are superbly illustrated by leading British fantasy artist Jim Cawthorn who was the original Sojan illustrator; he has provided us with a new set of illustrations created especially for this book.

Credits for the reprinted material are as follows: *The Secret Life of Elric of Melniboné* – CAMBER (1964), WEIRD FANTASY (1969); *The Stone Thing* – TRIODE (1975); *The Dying Castles* – NEW WORLDS No. 200 (1970); *Elric* – NIEKAS (1963); CRUCIFIED TOAD (1974). Jim Cawthorn's archetypal illustration for *Dek of Noothar* is reprinted from SATELLITE (1958) and truly captures the atmosphere of the original Sojan *œuvre*. The splash 'Elric' illustration is reprinted from Jim Cawthorn's definitive pictorial adaptation of Elric, STORMBRINGER, published 1976 by Savoy Books. The Sojan (and related) material first appeared in TARZAN ADVENTURES between the period August 1957–September 1958 (issues Vol. 7, No. 22–Vol. 8, No. 23) and corresponds roughly to the period during which the magazine was under Moorcock's editorial control.

THE STONE THING
(1975)

A TALE OF STRANGE PARTS

Out of the dark places; out of the howling mists; out of the lands without sun; out of Ghonorea came tall Catharz, with the moody sword Oakslayer in his right hand, the cursed spear Bloodlicker in his left hand, the evil bow Deathsinger on his back together with his quiver of fearful rune-fletched arrows, Heartseeker, Goregreedy, Soulsnatcher, Orphanmaker, Eyeblinder, Sorrowsower, Beanslicer, and several others.

Where his right eye should have been there was a jewel of slumbering scarlet whose colour sometimes shifted to smouldering blue, and in the place of his left eye was a many-faceted crystal, which pulsed as if possessed of independent life. Where Catharz had once had a right hand, now a thing of iron, wood and carved amethyst sat upon his stump; nine-fingered, alien, cut by Catharz from the creature who had sliced off his own hand. Catharz' left hand was at first merely gauntleted, but when one looked further it could be observed that the gauntlet was in fact a many jointed limb of silver, gold and lapis lazuli, but as Catharz rode by, those who saw him pass remarked not on the murmuring sword in his right hand, not on the whispering spear in his left hand, not on the whining bow upon his back or the grumbling arrows in the quiver; neither did they remark on his right eye of slumbering scarlet, his left eye of pulsing crystal, his nine-fingered right hand, his shining metallic left hand; they saw only the fearful foot of Cwlwwymwn which throbbed in the stirrup at his mount's right flank.

SOJAN

The foot of the Aching God, Cwlwwymwn Rootripper, whose ambition upon the old and weary Earth had been to make widows of all wives; Cwlwwymwn the Striker, whose awful feet had trampled whole cities when men had first made cities; Cwlwwymwn of the Last Ones, Last of the Last Ones, who had been driven back to his island domain on the edge of the world, beyond the Western Ice, and who now came limping after Catharz screaming out for vengeance, demanding the return of his foot, sliced from his leg by Oakslayer so that Catharz might walk again and continue upon his doom-laden quest, bearing weapons which were not his protection but his burden, seeking consolation for the guilt which ate at his soul since it was he who had been responsible for the death of his younger brother, Forax the Golden, for the death of his niece, Libia Gentleknee, for the living death of his cousin, Wertigo the Unbalanced, seeking the whereabouts of his lost love, Cyphila the Fair, who had been stolen from him by his arch-enemy, the wizard To'me'ko'op'r, most powerful, most evil, most lustful of all the great sorcerors of this magic-clouded world.

And there were no friends here to give aid to Catharz God-foot. He must go alone, with shuddering terror before him and groaning guilt behind him, and Cwlwwymwn, screaming, vengeful, limping Cwlwwymwn, following always.

And Catharz rode on, rarely stopping, scarcely ever dismounting, anxious to claim his own vengeance on the sorcerer, and the foot of Cwlwwymwn, Last of the Last Ones, was heavy on him, as well it might be for it was at least eighteen inches longer than his left foot and naked, for he had had to abandon his boot when he had found that it did not fit. Now Cwlwwymwn possessed the boot; it was how he had known that Catharz was the mortal who had stolen his green, seventeen-clawed limb, attaching it by fearful sorcery to the flesh of his leg. Catharz' left leg was not of flesh at all, but of lacquered cork, made for him by the People of the World Beneath the Reefs, when he had aided them in their great fight against the Gods of the Lowest Sea.

The sun had stained the sky a livid crimson and had sunk below the horizon before Catharz would allow himself a brief rest and it was just before dark that he came in sight of a small stone cottage, sheltered beneath terraces of glistening limestone, where he hoped he might find food, for he was very hungry.

Knocking upon the door he called out :

"Greetings, I come in friendship, seeking hospitality, for I am called Catharz the Melancholy, who carries the curse of Cwlwwymwn Rootripper upon him, who has many enemies and no friends, who slew his brother, Forax the Golden, and caused the death of Libia Gentleknee, famous for her beauty, and who seeks his lost love Cyphila the Fair, prisoner of the wizard To'me'ko'op'r, and who has a great and terrible doom upon him."

The door opened and a woman stood there. Her hair was the silver of a spiderweb in the moonlight, her eyes were the deep gold found at the centre of a beehive, her skin had the pale, blushing beauty of the tea-rose. "Welcome, stranger," said she. "Welcome to all that is left of the home of Lanoli, whose father was once the mightiest in these parts."

And, upon beholding her, Catharz forgot Cyphila the Fair, forgot that Cwlwwymwn Rootripper limped after him still, forgot that he had slain his brother, his niece, and betrayed his cousin, Wertigo the Unbalanced.

"You are very beautiful, Lanoli," he said.

"Ah," said she, "that is what I have learned. But beauty such as mine can only thrive if it is seen and it has been so long since anyone came to these lands."

"Let me help your beauty thrive," he said.

Food was forgotten, guilt was forgotten, fear was forgotten as Catharz divested himself of his sword, his spear, his bow and his arrows and walked slowly into the cottage. His gait was a rolling one, for he still bore the burden that was the foot of the Last of the Last Ones, and it took him some little time to pull it through the door, but at length he stood inside and had closed the door behind him and had taken her in his arms and had pressed his lips to hers.

"Oh, Catharz," she breathed. "Catharz!"

It was not long until they stood naked before one another. Her eyes travelled over his body and it was plain that the eyes of scarlet and of crystal were lovely to her, that she admired his silver hand and his nine-fingered hand, that even the great foot of Cwlwwymwn was beautiful in her sight. But then her eyes, shy until now, fell upon that which lay between his legs, and those eyes widened a little, and she blushed. Her lovely lips framed a question, but he moved forward as swiftly as he could and embraced her again.

"How?" she murmured. "How, Catharz?"

"It is a long tale and a bloody one," he whispered, "of rivalry and revenge, but suffice to say that it ended in my father, Xympwll the Cruel, taking a terrible vengeance upon me. I fled from his court into the wastes of Grxiwynn, raving mad, and it was there that the tribesmen of Velox found me and took me to the Wise Man of Oorps in the mountains beyond Katatonia. He nursed me and carved that for me. It took him two years, and all through those two years I remained raving, living off dust and dew and roots, as he lived. The engravings had mystical significance, the runes contain the sum of his great wisdom, the tiny pictures show all that there is to show of physical love. Is it not beautiful? More beautiful than that which it has replaced?"

Her glance was modest; she nodded slowly.

"It is indeed, very beautiful," she agreed. And then she looked up at him and he saw that tears glistened in her eyes. "But did it *have* to be made of Sandstone?"

"There is little else," he explained sadly, "in the mountains beyond Katatonia."

(From *The Outcast of Kitzoprenia* Volume 67 in *The History of the Purple Poignard*)

THE DYING CASTLES

(1970)

The horseman came riding through the pines with a gun in his hand.

I said: "Take it straight, baby," and moved out of the way. There was no sweat there, none at all.

Jewelled towers raised themselves above the horizon, and they were splendid. Mudwasps droned by the river. Light flashed in the city, light glittered on the flank beneath my thigh.

The gunman put down his gun. "You headed that way?"

"I'm taking it the way I told you to take it. There's the road." I motioned toward the gate; it was far away between the hills. O, so jewelled! Think, if you can see here, a man could stretch out and sleep on any face.

Sweetly, with considerable charitas, he bent and touched my nose. "Cosy," he said, and laughed. From his backside a sound issued. He rode on, the stink of his fart drifting through the pines. I flipped my cigarette into the ditch, turned and began to run towards the city.

(Glad Ladies, Kind Men: the castle and lands of Larne are fallen.)

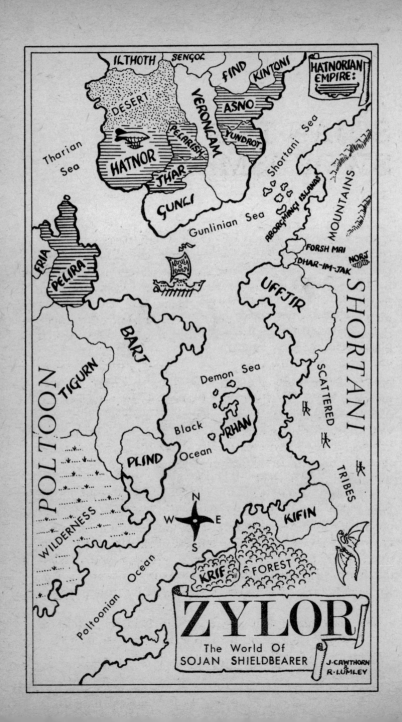

SOJAN THE SWORDSMAN

(1957)

A myat trotted peacefully across the broad, seemingly never-ending plain which made up the landscape as far as it was possible to see. No sound issued from the cloven hoofs, muffled by the moss-like substance which clothed the ground in a mantle of vivid colour – purple, green and yellow, with a trace of crimson or violet here and there. Nothing grew upon that plain. It was a wilderness, barren, deserted – the greatest desert on the planet of Zylor.

A wandering warror sat astride the myat's broad back. At his steed's side hung a shield, a virtually unknown accoutrement on Zylor, but the tribe to which Sojan belonged had perfected it as a valuable asset. The beast upon which he rode was a big, sturdy animal. From both sides of its huge head grew long sharp horns, curving outward. More like a reptile than a mammal, its head tapered like a snake's, its tail was thick and it, too, tapered.

Sojan was clothed in a bright blue jerkin reaching to his knees, his legs were bare and tough boots of myat hide were upon his feet, reaching to about two inches from his knees. Over the jerkin was a leather harness of simple design – two straps across his shoulders, coming to the waist and attached to a broad belt whereon hung his weapons – a sword, a dirk, long and sharp, and a holster containing his big, round-butted, air-pistol.

The mercenary's hair was long and held by a fillet of leather. At the back of his big saddle were two saddle-bags, a container of water and, rolled across these, his crimson cloak.

The man himself was tall, broad-shouldered and slim-waisted with smooth muscles rippling beneath his jerkin. The perfect fighting-man, keen-eyed and wary.

Suddenly Sojan caught a flash of marble to the west and knew that he had sighted Vermlot, the capital city of Hatnor, the greatest warrior nation of a warrior world. A rich city, was Vermlot, rich in fighting-men and weapons of war, rich in terms of gold, rich in beauty and splendour.

As he neared the city walls a guard bade him halt and state his business.

"I come in peace," he cried, "to offer my sword, my loyalty and my life to his Imperial Highness, the War Lord of Hatnor. I am a mercenary, my only possessions are the clothes I wear, the weapons I carry and the myat I ride. I have travelled half a world to offer my services to your ruler!"

He was admitted to the city and made his way to one of the many taverns situated within the protection of the mighty walls. His strange protective weapon aroused much interest. A certain warrior made mock of him and his shield.

"Oh!" he laughed. "What a brave mercenary! He has travelled half a world – to give us his protection – for with his great shield in front of him he will be able to withstand all our enemies. Perhaps he cannot fight without it. That's so, is it not, mercenary?"

Sojan halted and gazed up at the man who was leaning against a pillar on the balcony above.

Grimly, quietly, he spoke, but his tones were cold and his words were acid.

"I do not like your attitude," he said. "And I like your words less. Draw your sword – if you know how to use it – and defend yourself! Perhaps you will be hiding behind the shield before I have finished with you!"

The warrior stiffened and his face flushed: he put one hand on the balcony rail and vaulted into the street below, drawing his long 'vilthor', a sabre-like weapon, as he did so.

Sojan unslung his shield from the myat and drew his own

long blade. The warrior of the Palace struck first, aiming a wicked slash at Sojan's legs with his curved vilthor but the mercenary from Ilthoth jumped high in the air and attacked the other with a weaving arc of steel, driving him further and further back. Then the man saw his chance and slashed at an exposed limb of the mercenary's, but was too slow. There was a dull thud as the sword hit and rebounded from the shield, then he was made to duck beneath a vicious slash from Sojan.

The Vermlotian slowly lost ground until with a flick of his wrist Sojan disarmed his opponent. Then, from a second storey window a figure dropped, first to the balcony of the first storey and from there to the ground. He removed his cloak and, with a smile upon his lips, came forward with drawn sword.

"I fancy you will not disarm me so quickly."

This time Sojan was not so lucky for the newcomer was as quick as the proverbial cobra. His sword weaved an invisible circle around Sojan's guard and the newcomer soon had him at his mercy. Before he knew it, the mercenary's sword flew from his grasp and clattered to the earth, ten feet away.

"Yield?" questioned the victor.

"I yield," panted he. "You are a great fighter. Who are you, sir?"

"Perhaps you *have* heard of me," smiled his late adversary, "I am Nornos Kad, War Lord of the Imperial Empire of Hatnor!"

"Sir," said Sojan with a bow, "I, who came to enlist in your service and offer my aid to you, begin by fighting you. I crave your forgiveness."

Nornos Kad laughed, "Never mind, you did very well against my warrior here. To best him is a test indeed and I feel that I would do well to enlist your services." He signed to a servant who was waiting in a doorway. "Come, you will be my guest until I have need of you. Here, Oumlat, take Sojan to one of the best guest rooms and see that he is well looked after."

For a week or so Sojan enjoyed the privileges of the Royal

Guest until one morning a messenger came to say that Nornos Kad had asked for him.

"I summoned you, Sojan," Nornos Kad said, when they were alone, "because you are to accompany me on a journey. Our mission is to take Il-that, princess of Sengol, back to her father's country. I desire to bring Sengol into the Hatnorian alliance without bloodshed if possible and the king would think well of it if his daughter was personally escorted home by the War Lord himself. You had better prepare your weapons and be ready to move from your quarters by dawn tomorrow."

Ten warships, heavily armed with Hatnorian air-guns which worked on the simple principle of compressed air, with a range of over half a mile, and the Royal Airship, were ready to take to the air early the next morning. They rose majestically, hovered for a few moments, and then, with motors purring, the great gas-bags veered off towards Sengol which lay far to the north.

Within three or four hours they had crossed the outermost boundary of Hatnor and her satellites and were winging their way at a steady eighty miles an hour over Veronlam, a country which owed no allegiance to Hatnor and which, although fearing the mighty Empire, was constantly stirring up petty strife between the minor Hatnorian nations. They had nearly reached the border of Veronlam when the soft purr of motors was heard and a shell whistled past them and exploded in their rear air container.

"Veronlam pirates!" yelled the fore-gunner.

Quickly the small fleet formed a protective barrier about the Royal ship. One airship was hit a dozen times in as many different places and hurtled downwards, flames roaring from the gas-bag and the crew jumping overboard rather than die in the flames.

Nornos Kad realised at once that to fight against so many would soon end in disaster for his fleet, and he ordered them to turn about and flee back to Hatnor. He decided to rely upon his speedier engines to aid them rather than their powerful guns.

The Hatnorian fleet circled and fled. Nornos Kad was the last to leave the battle and hastily turned about to follow his ships. But alas, it was too late, for three well-aimed shots in their main tank sent them spiralling slowly to earth to land with a sickening crash amidst a tangle of red-hot girders and flaming fabric. Being on the platform of the ship Nornos Kad, Sojan and Il-that were flung clear of the main wreckage, to lie stunned.

Sojan did not know how long it was he lay amidst the wreckage of the Royal Airship, but when he awoke it was dawn. He knew that none could have escaped if they had been trapped in the wreckage but nevertheless he spent a fruitless two hours searching for his companions — all he found were two or three charred corpses but none lived. Convinced that his companions were dead he took the only unbroken water bottle and set off in the direction of Hatnor. Sojan's eye caught the gleam of white stone far to the south of his position. With a sigh of relief he began to walk quickly towards the gleam which grew soon into a patch and from that into a city, its walls towering fifty paces in places. Knowing that he was still probably in Veronlam he knew that it would be useless to try to gain admission on the strength of his allegiance to Nornos Kad the War Lord. Stripping himself of his Hatnorian Navy-Cloak and also his Navy-type gauntlets he stood arrayed as when he had first entered Hatnor, as a mercenary swordsman.

He easily gained admittance to the city of Quentos as mercenaries were always welcome to swell the ranks of any army.

"By Mimuk, friend, you're the third to pass through these gates this day," the guard said, as he was allowed to enter the city.

"The third. That's strange is it not guard?" replied Sojan, "three people in one day! Mimuk, you must be joking!"

"I joke not, friend mercenary, strange as it seems two others have preceded you and one of them was a woman. Our warriors found them near the wreck of an airship. Some say the ones we captured were Nornos Kad himself and Il-that, daughter of Hugor of Sengol. Two prizes indeed if it be the truth."

Sojan strode off in the direction indicated by the friendly guard.

Arriving at the tavern he hired a room and ordered himself a meal. Finishing his repast, he was horrified to find that the only money he had was that of Hatnor. If he tried to pass this he knew that the suspicions of the keeper of the tavern would be instantly aroused. What should he do? He had brought nothing with him to the tavern save his sword, shield and poinard and the clothes he wore. He reasoned that the only chance he stood was to try and slip quietly out of the door before the proprietor spotted him and ordered him to pay his bill.

Just as he thought he had reached the safety of the street a hand fell on his shoulder and the leering face of the landlord was brought close to his.

"Going so soon, my lord? Methinks you would like to stay and sample some more of our victuals before you make your – er – *hasty* departure," he said with ponderous sarcasm. "Now pay up or my men'll make sure you pay for your meal – in blood!"

"You threaten me, by Mimuk!" cried Sojan, his easily roused temper getting the better of him. "You dare threaten me! Draw your weapon!"

"Hey, Tytho, Zatthum, Wanrim – come and save me from this murdering bilker!" cried the keeper of the tavern in terror.

Instantly three ruffians appeared in the narrow doorway and, drawing their blades, rushed at Sojan, causing him to release his grasp upon the unfortunate man and turn to face this new danger.

Zatthum went down in the first minute with an inch of steel marking its path through his heart. The remaining two were not so easily defeated. Back and forth across the narrow street the three fought, sparks flying from their blades, the clang of their weapons resounding upon the rooftops. Sojan was marked in a dozen places, but his adversaries were bleeding in as many as he was. With a quick thrust, a parry and another thrust the mercenary succeeded in dispatching the second man. Now only Tytho was left. Sojan allowed himself to be headed off and the man edged him completely round so that they were now retracing their path. With a mighty effort Sojan, who was still tired after his narrow escape from the airship, gathered his remaining strength together and made a vicious lunge in Tytho's direction. He cried out in pain when Sojan's blade found the muscles of his left arm, but did not relax his grip upon his own sword. Again Sojan was forced further back towards the gaping crowd which had collected outside the tavern. His shield saved him from the thrust designed to end the fight but he knew he could not last longer for he was rapidly tiring. Suddenly his foot caught in the trappings of one of the dead men's harnesses and he fell backwards across the corpse. A grim smile graced Tytho's face as he raised his sword to deliver the final thrust.

"*Kill him, Tytho, kill him,*" the crowd roared in frenzied bloodlust.

Sojan, entangled in the harness of the man he had slain, tried to rise but was stopped from doing so by a shove from Tytho's booted foot.

The hireling raised his sword again and the crowd leaned forward.

Suddenly there was a disturbance at one end of the street and the crowd quickly began to disperse. As it did so, Tytho saw the City Patrol, scourge of the city thieves, was the cause of the crowd's disappearance. Looking hurriedly about him for a way of escape he found none; he dropped his sword and began to run, foolishly, *along* the street.

The leader of the Patrol raised his pistol. There was the slight hiss of escaping air and the running hireling gave a short cry, threw up his arms, stumbled and dropped on the cobbles of the street.

"What's happening here?"

By this time Sojan had disentangled himself from the harness of his late opponent and was standing, legs a'sprawl, hand to head.

"You've saved my life, sir!" he gasped. "These ruffians attacked me for my money. I succeeded in killing two but unfortunately became tangled up with this fellow." He indicated the body. "Tytho was about to finish me when you arrived!"

The leader laughed. "You certainly accounted very well for yourself," he said, "these three are among the worst of the type with whom we have to contend. Ruthless murderers, perfect swordsmen." Again he laughed, "Or almost perfect. You did us a service and I am grateful."

He surveyed Sojan's bloodstained and tattered clothing.

"You're a stranger here are you not?" he enquired, "a mercenary swordsman, perhaps?"

"Yes, I am named Sojan – they nickname me 'Shieldbearer' as I use this." Sojan pointed to his shield.

"Well, Sojan Shieldbearer, how would you like to bear a shield and wield a sword in the Patrol?"

Instantly Sojan saw his chance. If he could get a post in the organised militia of the city, he might be able to contact his imprisoned friends.

"It has always been my ambition to serve in the Veron-lamite Guard," he lied, "but to become a member of the great Patrol is a chance for which I had not dared hope."

"Then come with us and we'll enlist you immediately. And," he added, "get you a decent jerkin and harness."

Before he could become a full-fledged Patrolman, Sojan had to undergo a course of basic training. When this was finished, his duties were to Patrol, with his men, a certain section of the city, and arrest any thieves, footpads or similar wrongdoers. The 'justice' was rough indeed and was not appreciated by the population. All the time he heard rumours and from these rumours he gleaned that Nornos Kad and Il-that were imprisoned somewhere in the Prison of Zholun – a mighty towered building situated near the centre of the city. Sojan knew well that the Patrol's duties included patrolling the prison and acting as guards to "special" prisoners – and he was hoping that he would be given this assignment soon.

Sure enough, one day his hopes were fulfilled and he was assigned to guard a section of Zholun Prison.

With his eyes wide open, Sojan learned where the two were imprisoned.

"One is in the East tower – the other in the West. Nornos Kad lies in the East tower," a guard told Sojan one night after Sojan had plied him with enough ale to get him drunk.

Sojan had to work fast; there were rumours that his friends were to die by the sword in two days' time.

His first loyalty was to Nornos Kad. He contrived to enter the East tower wherein Nornos Kad was imprisoned. Stealthily he made his way to the metal-studded door of the cell.

"Nornos Kad," he whispered.

He heard the rattle of chains and through the bars of the door saw his chieftain's handsome face, drawn and pale through lack of food and sleep.

"Sojan!" exclaimed the War Lord. "I thought you died in the crash!"

"I am alive and here to save you if I can. I was assigned to guard the West wing so it will be more difficult – however I shall try and get the keys. Until I return – have hope!"

And with that Sojan crept back along the gloomy passage. On return he found that the Patrolman on duty was talking to someone. He waited until the man had left and then walked into the little room which was being used to house guards.

"Hullo, Stontor," cried Sojan, "what's up?"

Stontor looked worried, "It's my wife, Sojan, she's been taken ill and I can't leave my post."

Sojan saw his chance.

"Well, you go and help her," he said. "I'll stay here until you get back. Don't worry."

"Thanks a lot, Sojan, you're a friend indeed. Here are the

keys – shouldn't think there'll be much doing tonight." And with that he picked up his cloak and ran down the long passage.

Hastily Sojan picked up the keys and ran back to Nornos Kad's cell. Unlocking the door he helped Nornos Kad from his chains.

"I was lucky – a coincidence – guard's wife ill – but the main trouble will be getting out of the city," he panted, as he unlocked the heavy padlocks.

Together they returned to the guards' room. Here Sojan left Nornos Kad. Then he made his way back to the West wing where it was a simple matter to get the princess from her cell. Silently they returned to Nornos Kad.

Keeping to the sidestreets and the shadows, the three sped along towards the city gates.

Suddenly Nornos Kad hissed, "Stop! Stop, Sojan, there may be an easier way." He pointed to a flat area dotted with hangers and anchored airships. "With one of those we would have a better chance of escaping."

"But how?" enquired Sojan.

Again Nornos Kad pointed. "You see that small ship nearest to us – the one anchored down by a couple of ropes?" The ship of which he was speaking was fifteen feet above them, held to the ground by anchors attached to heavy ropes. "With luck we could gain the ship and climb the ropes."

Stealthily they padded along the side of the field, keeping well into the shadows all the time. A single guard lolled on the ground. Sojan crept behind him and, reversing his pistol, knocked the man unconscious.

With Sojan's and Nornos Kad's help, Il-that was able to climb the rope and they boarded the ship. As they clambered over the rail a light suddenly appeared from one of the cabins and an armed man appeared on deck. He was followed by three others.

"Mimuk!" he cried, "what have we here?"

There was no time for words and, handing Nornos Kad his long dirk and Il-that his pistol, Sojan drew his sword, and engaged the man and his companions. Nornos Kad was close behind him. Back and forth across the narrow deck the six men fought, and the four crewmen were no mean battlers. Nornos Kad, weak from his sojourn in Zholun Prison, still put up a good fight. Together they succeeded in killing two of their opponents – but the other two were better swordsmen. The clash of steel echoed across the silent field. Sojan was blinded by the sudden flash of a searchlight and taking advantage of this, his opponent cut past his guard and made a painful gash in his side. The pain was like fire and Sojan could barely restrain himself from crying out. He stumbled to the deck and with a cry of triumph the crewman raised his sword. A sudden hiss and a strangled gasp and he collapsed over Sojan. Turning his head he saw Il-that with the pistol in her hand.

"Thanks," was all he could say as he struggled to his feet and ran to help Nornos Kad.

While Nornos Kad threw the bodies overboard, Sojan started the engines. Below them they heard shouts of a Patrol and two searchlights were now levelled on the swaying airship. Soon they heard cries as the bodies of the crewmen were found.

With two sword strokes Nornos Kad cut the anchoring ropes and the ship rose swiftly into the air. There was a coughing roar and the propellers began to turn. The searchlights followed them; all around them shells whistled.

Suddenly, behind them, they saw that three battlecruisers of the fastest and heaviest type had risen to follow them.

"More speed Sojan, more speed!" cried Nornos Kad, "make for Sengol, it's nearer."

With a glance at the compass, Sojan turned the ship's nose towards the North. Nearer and nearer came the battlecruisers, guns popping softly. Il-that, a true daughter of a warrior king, climbed into the gunner's rear-seat and aimed the guns of their own ship at the pursuing cruisers. She pressed the triggers and the twin muzzles of the gun gave a jerk, a hiss, and there was an explosion. What all a gunner's skill could not easily have accomplished, Il-that had done with luck – brought down a cruiser in its most vulnerable spot – the main gas-bag. Flames roared from the fabric and the ship lost height. Faster and faster it went as the earth pulled it downwards. The engines roaring to the last it crashed with a flash of orange and crimson flame. But the other two ships had still to be accounted for and Il-that was not so lucky this time.

For two hours the chase continued, neither gaining and all the time the shells from the Veronlam craft were getting closer and closer as the gunner perfected his aim.

"They will catch us soon," cried Il-that, who still sat in the rear-gunner's seat, "they seem to be drawing closer!"

"Then we shall have to land and hope that we're not still in Veronlam," yelled Nornos Kad above the shrieking wind.

"It will be a long time for us to do so, sir," Sojan told Nornos Kad, "we have no anchors, and to release the gas in the gas-bag would mean that while we lost height we should also lose speed."

"Then there's only one thing we can do!" cried the Emperor, "and that's this!" Raising his sword he cut deep into the nearest gas-bag. He was thrown to the deck as the contents rushed out and almost at once the ship began to drop, dangerously fast. The three stood by the side, ready to jump.

With a hard jolt the ship touched the ground, bumped along it, and stopped. Over the side the three companions went and ran over soft moss to the sheltering shadows of some rocks as the Veronlamite searchlights began to stab into the darkness.

But it was easy to hide in the rocks and the caves sheltered them when the Veronlams landed and made a vain search for them.

In the morning it was an easy matter to walk to the nearest Sengolian city and thence to the capital, where the king gratefully took his daughter and promised that Sengol would always be an ally to Hatnor.

(Original draft c. 1955)

MISSION TO ASNO

Motors purring, captains shouting orders, the rustle of the canvas gun-covers being drawn back, gay flags, flashing steel, flying cloaks of many hues; a Hatnorian war-fleet rose rapidly into the sky.

On the deck of the flagship stood a tall, strong figure – that of Sojan, nicknamed 'Shieldbearer', second in command to the great War Lord of Hatnor himself – Nornos Kad.

At his side was a long broadsword, upon his back his round shield; his right hand rested on the butt of his heavy air-pistol – an incredibly powerful weapon. Clad in a jerkin of sky-blue, a divided kilt of deep crimson and boots of dark leather, over his shoulder his leathern war-harness, he was the typical example of a Zylorian mercenary, whose love of bright garb was legendary.

The great war-fleet was destined for Asno – a country far to the north of Hatnor where the king, so the spies told, was raising an army of mercenaries to attack Yundrot – a colony of the Hatnorian Empire.

To stop a major war, Nornos Kad decided to send a mighty fleet to crush the attack before it was started. Having other business, he assigned Sojan to take his place and instructed him to completely wipe out any signs of an attack.

Only too pleased at the chance of battle, Sojan had readily assented and was now on his way – the entire fleet under his command.

Soon the fleet was winging its way over Asno – a land of snow and ice, fierce beasts, great tracts of uninhabited ice-fields – uninhabited, that is, by *civilised* beings.

In another hour it would be over Boitil, the capital city.

"Gunners, take your positions!" Sojan roared through cupped hands and picking up a megaphone – for there was no radio on Zylor – shouted the same orders, which went from ship to ship until every gunner was seated in his seat, guns loaded and ready for firing.

"Drop two hundred feet!" Sojan roared again to the steersman, and repeated these orders to the other captains, who in turn shouted them to their own steersmen.

"Prepare hand weapons and fasten down loose fixtures, check gas-bag coverings, every man to position!" Sojan shouted when the ships had all dropped two hundred feet.

"Slow speed!" The ships slowed into 'second-speed'.

In Zylorian naval terms there are five speeds: 'Speed No. 1' is fastest possible, 'Speed No. 2' is a fifth of this slower, and so on. When a commander gives the order to slow when travelling at Speed No. 1, the ship automatically adjusts to Speed No. 2; if going at No. 2 and told to slow, it changes to No. 3.

Now they were over the outskirts of the city, dropping lower and lower until Sojan thought they would touch the very towers of Boitil, scanning the squares and flying-fields for signs of the army. Halfway over the city a message was passed to Sojan that a great army camp had been spotted – just on the outskirts of the city. At the same time someone yelled for him to look, and doing so he saw that a fleet almost as large as his own was rising from flying-fields all over the vast city.

"Prepare for battle!" he shouted.

As one, the safety catches of the guns were pushed off.

"Shoot as you will!" Sojan ordered.

There was a muffled 'pop' and the hiss of escaping air as the explosive shells of the Hatnorian craft were sent on their mission of destruction. Almost at once the enemy retaliated.

Two Hatnorian ships, one only slightly damaged, the other a mass of roaring yellow and blue flame, dropped earthwards.

For twelve hours the great air-battle was fought, developing into ship-to-ship duels as the opposing sides became mixed. Bit by bit the battle moved southwards until it was over the great ice wastes.

But expert handling of their craft, superior marksmanship and a slightly superior weight of numbers on the part of the Hatnorian fleet was slowly but surely weakening the Asnogian fleet. Sojan, now with a gun mounted on the officer's platform, was taking an active part in the battle. His uncanny ability to hit almost whatever he aimed at was taking great toll. Everywhere ships were hurtling earthwards, crashing in an inferno of flame, or merely bouncing gently when a gas-bag was only slightly punctured.

At last, one by one, the enemy began to flee. The other ships, seeing their companions escape, disengaged and followed them. The hired ships, manned mainly by mercenaries, flew in every direction but that of Asno, while the Asnogian craft turned and headed for their home base. In this direction went the Hatnorian fleet, re-forming to a close formation and turning to No. 1 speed. If they overtook a ship it was ruthlessly shot down; but half a dozen or so were lucky and escaped them. In three hours they were back over Asno and bombing the troop encampment with incendiaries until nothing remained of the great camp but smouldering fabric and twisted steel. Through the south gate of the city streamed forth ragged bands of hired soldiers, bent on escaping while they could. The planned attack on a Hatnorian colony had not even begun. A just reprisal on Nornos Kad's part. A reprisal carried out in full by Sojan. But his business was not finished and, landing on part of an undamaged airfield, Sojan ordered the frightened commanding officer to take him to King Tremorn of Asno.

"I bring a message from my Emperor!" he cried when he was in the vast chamber which housed the king's court. All around him stood courtiers and servants, worried and anxious to hear his terms. Great pillars supported the roof and brilliant tapestries hung from the ceiling. Murals on the walls depicted scenes of battles, on land, water and in the air.

"Speak your message," ordered the king. "What are your terms? I admit that I am beaten! For the present!" he added.

"For all time, sir, while a member of the Nornos family sits on the throne of Hatnor!" Sojan replied. "Now, do you wish to hear my terms?"

"Speak!"

"The first is that you acknowledge allegiance to Hatnor and pay a tribute of five hundred young men to train in our armies every tenth year. The second is that you disband any army you still have, save for policing your city. On signs of attack, you will notify the Empire, who will come to your aid. As a member of the Empire you will be subject to all laws and trading terms of the Empire and in times of major war shall enlist two-thirds of your fighting strength in the armies of Hatnor and the remaining third if called upon. You will not make war-ships or weapons of war, save hand weapons, for your own use, but all war-ships and arms shall be sent direct to the capital. Do you recognise these terms?"

The king paused and, turning to his *major domo*, whispered a few words to him. The man nodded.

"Yes, I recognise your terms," he sighed.

"Then sign your name and oath to this document and seal it with your royal seal. Upon the breaking of your word, the lapse shall be punished according to the magnitude."

Sojan handed the paper to a courtier who carried it to the king. The act of bowing to a king is unknown upon the planet Zylor, instead the subject places his right hand upon his heart to signify complete allegiance.

So it was that Sojan achieved his purpose. But more adventures were yet to come before he could return to his palace at Hatnor.

SOJAN, SWORDSMAN OF ZYLOR!

(1957)

REVOLT IN HATNOR

"Sojan, Sojan!" the call rang across the clear Zylorian sky as a small scout-ship veered towards the larger warship, the flagship of Sojan, second-in-command to the War Lord of Hatnor – Nornos Kad.

"Who are you?" Sojan's lieutenant roared through a megaphone.

"I bring urgent tidings from the court of Nornos Kad – the land is in turmoil!"

"Come alongside," the man roared.

As the scout-ship drew alongside, an armed man jumped from it and rushed up the ladder to the platform whereon Sojan stood.

"Sojan! While the fleet has been at war, revolution has swept through the land. Nornos Kad has been deposed and a tyrant sits on the throne of Hatnor. There is a price upon your head and upon the heads of all whom you command.

"Flee now, Sojan, while you have the chance. Trewin the Upstart controls the city and half the Empire. The other half is in a state of unrest, unsure whether to support one Emperor or another!"

"I cannot flee while my Emperor rots in chains – tell me, who still cries 'Loyalty to the Nornos family?'"

"None, openly, Sojan. A few are suspected, but they are still powerful nobles and even Trewin dare not arrest them without cause."

Sojan's face became grim and he clenched his hand upon his sword hilt.

"Lun!" he cried. "Order the fleet to turn about and adjust to Speed 1!"

A look of surprise crossed his lieutenant's face. "We're not running, Sojan?"

"Do as I say!"

"Turn about and adjust to Speed 1!" Lun shouted through his megaphone.

At once the great fleet turned gracefully about and adjusted, speed by speed, until it was flying at maximum speed. There were puzzled looks in the eyes of many of Sojan's captains, but they obeyed his order.

"Tell them to set a course for Poltoon," he ordered Lun. Lun did so and soon every ship was heading south – to the steaming jungles and burning deserts of the Heat Lands.

"Why do we sail for Poltoon, Sojan?" asked Lun.

But Sojan's only reply was, "You will see," and he resumed his earnest conversation with the messenger who had brought him the news.

On the third day they were sailing at No. 1 speed over a vast belt of jungle, seemingly impenetrable. But Sojan's eyes, less atrophied by civilised living, caught what he had been looking for – a patch of green, lighter than the dark green which predominated.

"STOP!" he roared. "Stop and hover – no one is to drop anchor."

The flying machines of the Zylorian nations are usually very similar to our airships. The gondola is supported by steel hawsers depending from the main gas-bag. The propeller is adjustable and can be slung either fore or aft of the ship – it is usually slung aft. They are steered by two methods, a rudder aft plus manipulation of the propeller. A normal sized warship usually mounts five guns – two very powerful ones fore and aft, a smaller one on the captain's platform and two mounted in a platform on top of the huge gas-bag. The gunners reach this platform by means of ladders from the deck to the platform. This position is extremely dangerous and if ever the gas-bag is hit it is unlikely that a gas-bag gunner could ever escape.

The ships stopped as ordered and while they waited, Sojan had his ship drop downwards, nearer and nearer to the little patch of green which became a small clearing, just large enough to land one ship, but for a fleet of over fifty ships to land here was impossible. With a slight bump the ship dropped to the ground and the anchor was thrown into the soft grass. Sojan ordered that the gas-bags be deflated. They could always be inflated again as every ship carried a large supply of gas-cylinders.

Now the ship was only a third of the size and was dragged into the undergrowth which was not at all thick. Sojan told his crew of eight to get to work and chop down all the small growth but to leave the huge forest giants standing. This they did and very soon the clearing widened and as it did so a new ship dropped down until the fifty were all deflated and covering a large area of ground under the trees. The cabins made excellent living quarters so there was no difficulty about housing the men. Rations were also plentiful and a spring of fresh water was nearby.

"I know this part of the country well," Sojan told his men that night, "the inhabitants are for the most part friendly. While they are not civilised, they are not savages and I believe that they will give us some help. But now we sleep and to-morrow we shall rouse the tribes!"

Next morning, Sojan with a small party of his men set off for the village of his barbarian friends.

The chief greeted him warmly and was interested in Sojan's need for soldiers.

"You know me and my people, Soyin," he said, using the nearest Poltoonian equivalent of Sojan's name. "We all love to fight – and if there's a bit of loot thrown in, who's to say 'no'?"

"Then I can depend on you?"

"By all means – I shall form a council immediately and

35

recruit as many of my fellow chiefs as possible. Between us we should muster a few thousand fighting men."

By Zylorian standards, where most nations are comparatively small to Earth nations, a thousand men is quite a large number.

"Then have them ready by the third day, my friend," Sojan replied. "Blood will stain the usurper's robes before the month is gone!"

THE HORDES ATTACK

The day of the invasion was drawing nearer and Sojan began to work harder and harder in the training of his barbarian horde – the Poltoonians. Spies brought word that there was more and more unrest in the outlying provinces of Hatnor.

"The time is ripe to strike," Sojan told his captains and the wild chiefs. "We must invade now or our cause will be lost and we will never again have the opportunity to win Hatnor back from the usurper and restore Nornos Kad to his rightful throne!"

His airships, camouflaged by the mighty trees of the steaming Poltoonian jungle, were provisioned and ready to do battle. His captains were word-perfect in his plan of invasion. Everyone had his orders and knew how to carry them out.

A day later a horde, consisting of thousands of mounted barbarians led by Sojan himself, moved towards the North – and Hatnor!

Two days later, the faster moving airships rose into the air like a swarm of hornets armed with stings a hundred times more powerful. As they passed the horde, the ships slowed to minimum speed and followed, flying low, just above them. In another day they would arrive at the boundaries of Hatnor – and blood would run in the gutters of all who opposed them.

Sojan was sure that very little blood would flow as the army would be on his side. It was the criminal population, egged on by an evil and power-mad noble, who had risen and overthrown their Emperor while the bulk of his army was crushing a rebellion in an outer province.

There would always be unrest in any regime, Sojan knew this, but there was no cause for the people to grumble about their ruler. As always, the unrest had been caused by a power-seeker intent on turning a nation into a blood-bath for his own selfish ends.

Now the once happy people groaned beneath the tyrant's yoke, no man, woman or child could count themselves safe from his oppression.

Not only men made up the barbarian army, their maidens rode beside them, armed with knife, sword, shield and spear. In their left hands they carried charm sticks to keep their men and themselves from harm. Most of these girls were extremely beautiful and the armour they wore did not detract from their good looks in anyway, rather it enhanced them.

At last they reached the outer boundaries of the Empire and found little opposition here. It would be later, when news of their invasion reached the city of Hatnor, that the fighting would begin. Sojan was finding it difficult to keep the barbarians in order; they had decided that anyone could be slain as long as they got their loot. But after a council meeting with the chiefs he was sure that they would be reliable for a time.

Two days later found them at the gates of Vermlot, gates which were securely locked and guarded.

The barbarians were all for laying violent siege to the place, but Sojan realised that they could hold out for an eternity.

"You are forgetting our ships," he said, "we have the whole of the Hatnorian airforce under our control. They will not last as long as they hope!"

His flagship sailed gracefully down for him and then shot up again when he was aboard. Orders were shouted from ship to ship and the fleet dipped downwards towards the great city square. Aboard were hundreds of soldiers, the most reliable of the barbarian horde, and as soon as the ships reached the ground, not without some opposition, they swarmed from the ships and ran to engage the rather frightened militia who barred their way.

Wild cries, strangely woven banners raised against a background of flashing steel and muffled poppings of the air-pistols and rifles. It was impossible to use the heavier artillery.

Into the square they poured and soon it was impossible to tell friend or foe as the fighting surged back and forth, spreading outwards into the streets, into the very houses themselves. Attacked from the inside as well as at their walls, the tyrant's men were uncertain whom to attack and while they wavered, the barbarians took the opportunity to batter in one of the minor gateways and clamber over the inner wall.

The streets were slippery with blood, echoing with the ring of steel and the cries of the wounded.

Sojan was in front, hewing and hacking with his great blade, his long hair streaming behind him and a grim smile upon his lips. "To the Palace, to the Palace," he cried. "Take the Palace or our cause is lost!"

And, like a tidal wave, the army surged over their enemies in the direction of the great Palace. The doors would not open to their thunderous knocking so battering rams were brought in. As the main door flew open, Sojan and his men drew back in horror.

There stood Nornos Kad, their ruler, worn and in rags, a filthy stubble on his face. And surrounding him, a body of Trewin's personal guard. Behind them stood their leader.

"Come another step closer, Sojan, and I'll be forced to kill your precious Emperor!" he called.

Sojan and his men were in a quandary, what were they to do? It was checkmate, if not defeat, for them.

An idea sprang into Sojan's mind.

Aiming a pistol at Nornos Kad, he pulled the trigger. The Emperor fell to the ground with a moan and lay still.

"There, dog, I've done your dirty work for you!" he laughed.

In a rage Trewin fired blindly at Sojan. The Swordsman

flung himself to the ground and the bullet whistled by to catch one of his men in the shoulder.

Lifting his own pistol, Sojan fired twice. Trewin, in the act of fleeing up the staircase, flung up his arms and toppled down the great stairway, blood trickling from his mouth. He landed with a thud at the feet of his guards.

With a cry, Sojan, his sword glistening in the light of the torches suspended around the hall, charged for the astounded guards who, without thinking, threw down their weapons and fled.

Nornos Kad picked himself up from the floor with Sojan's help.

"A clever move, Sojan," he grinned, "but it took some clever shooting, too."

He examined the hole which Sojan's bullet had made in his coat.

"It was a minor risk, sir. If I had not taken it, the city would even now be in the hands of Trewin."

"At the moment it seems to be in the hands of your Poltoonian barbarians," laughed the War Lord. "Let us go to the rescue of our fellow countrymen."

Peace had come once more to Hatnor.

SOJAN AND THE SEA OF DEMONS

(1957)

THE PURPLE GALLEY

To describe the wonderful pageantry, the colours, the races and the myriad weapons which flashed in that great hall would be impossible. The gleaming white stones of the hall, hung with vivid tapestries of red, black, gold, yellow, orange, green and purple, almost reflected the equally scintillating colours of the uniforms and dresses of the men and women who stood before the throne of Nornos Kad.

But there was one uniform missing, one tall figure which should have been there was not, one sword did not flash in the great hall.

And the faces of the nobles were sad – for the missing man was Nornos Rique, Prince of Hatnor – the War Lord's son.

"My people," said Nornos Kad, softly and very sadly, "my son has been missing for thirteen days now and still no news of him or the Princess Asderma. Has any one *anything* to report – you, Sojan, have you found any traces of my son?"

"No, sire, although I have searched the whole nation. I can only conclude that your son is not in the Hatnorian Empire!"

"Then we must find him, Sojan! Take the men you require – and return with my son! If it is possible then you are the man to find him!"

The sun was just setting when a weary and travel-stained rider guided his myat into the small collection of stone and wooden buildings which was the border town of Erm. He had ridden for days, stopping only to eat and gather a few hours'

sleep when he could no longer stay awake. His clothes were good and were mainly made of durable hide. His weapons nestled in well-oiled sheaths and scabbards, his shield was covered with canvas. It was easy to see that here was the typical soldier of fortune – a Zylorian mercenary.

He dismounted at the small tavern and called through the door which was ajar.

"Hey there! Is there a stable for my animal and a bed for me?"

"Yes, my lord," came a woman's voice from the tavern and a girl of about eighteen appeared in the doorway. "Hey, Kerk!" she called. "Fetch a blanket for this gentleman's myat and take him to the stables!"

"This way my lord," said the battle-scarred veteran who came to do the woman's bidding. "What's trade like?" he added with a grin as they neared the wooden building which served as a stable for the beasts of the whole village.

"Not too bad," the mercenary smiled. "As long as men are men and their tempers are the same then I'll never be out of a job. There was an uprising in Hatnor some months ago. That was a good scrap if ever there was one!"

"Aye, I heard about it from another gentleman who came this way soon after it happened. Didn't say much, though – most untalkative type if you ask me! He wasn't a Hatnorian – nor a Northerner for that matter, that was easy to see!"

"What do you mean?" The mercenary was obviously interested; more than casually so.

"He was a Shortani man, you can't mistake 'em."

"Shortani's a big continent – did you hear him say what country in Shortani?"

"Wait a minute. I believe he did say something." The old man paused and tugged at his grizzled beard. He frowned, thinking hard. "Yes, I've got it – it was raining at the time. Like it does *most* of the time in these parts," Kerk laughed – "Never seems to stop it don't . . ."

"Yes," the mercenary was impatient, "but what did he say?"

"What? Oh, yes. The country. Well, *he* said, when he got here, that it was 'never like this in Uffjir'. Yes, that was it."

"Uffjir, hmmm, that's right on the farthest side of Shortani. And even then he may not have been returning there. It probably isn't anything but it seems strange for an Uffjirian to travel so far from his tropical lands, especially in winter. What did he look like, this man?"

"Oh! The usual type, you know. Small, a bit fat, wore one of them fancy jewelled swords which snaps as soon as you cross it with a good bit of Turani steel. Why, I remember when I was a young 'un – that would be a bit before your time. We didn't have none of them newfangled flying machines in *those* days, I can tell you. *We* had to do all our travelling by myat – or more likely on our feet . . ."

"Yes!" The mercenary was almost crying with impatience by this time. "But can you describe the Uffjirian?"

"Well, he had a *beard* if that's any good. And it was curled up a bit – looked as if he'd put oil on it. Wore fancy clothes, too, no good for travelling but expensive – yes, they were certainly expensive. He was a nobleman by the look of him – hired a whole crowd of the village men and they all went off together somewhere. They ain't back yet."

"Have you any idea where they went?"

"Only the direction. They went off in the opposite direction to the one from which you came. Mounted, too, and although they wouldn't admit it, every one of them has a sword hidden in his blankets. They can't fool *me*, I have to look after their myats!"

The myat had been rubbed down and was in his stable by this time, attended by the two men, one an aged veteran with over a hundred years of fighting behind him and the other equally a veteran with not much more than twenty years behind him. They lived short lives on Zylor for most men died of a sword thrust by the time they were seventy or eighty. Their life span of 120 years was rarely reached.

That night, the mercenary sat in the corner of the tavern,

drinking and cleaning his heavy pistol. There were two other visitors at the tavern. A young man of seventeen years or so and his father. They were friendly men and the mercenary and he found mutual ground in that they were both veterans of the Findian/Kintonian wars. The mercenary had fought for the Findians and the man – Orfil – had fought on the side of the Kintonians. But there was no bad feeling between the men for at that time Orfil had also been a mercenary. Now he was a merchant – dealing in precious jewels – and he and his son were travelling to Aborgmingi, a small group of islands in the Shortani Sea. The mining of precious stones was unknown there, he said, and he found it worth his while to travel the distance over land and sea to sell them as they obtained prices which were over five times as much as those in Fria, his own country.

"Ride with us," he invited, "there is always a greater amount of safety if there is a greater amount of men and I would be glad of your company."

"I ride towards Shortani," said Sojan, "but whether I shall for long depends on circumstances."

The merchant knew better than to ask what 'circumstances' they were for privacy means life on Zylor and those who ask too many needless questions are liable to find themselves in an alleyway keeping close company with a knife!

The three men retired to their respective rooms and the mercenary was glad to get some rest. Wearily he sank on to the not-so-soft bed and lay down to sleep.

In the morning he awoke at his accustomed hour and attempted to rise. He could not, for his hands were bound. He was strapped to the bed and the only thing he could move was his head. Looking down at him with a smile on his face was – Orfil the merchant, and his son. Only his 'son' had donned her skirts again and was an extremely pretty girl!

"Well, my nosy soldier, you've put your nose into one game too many this time!" laughed Orfil, who seemed to be enjoying a great joke. The girl behind him was not so amused. Her whole bearing was tense and the hand that gripped the pistol at her side gleamed white at the knuckles.

"Perhaps I should introduce myself," continued the man, "my name *is* Orfil. I am the Captain of the Spies Guild in Rhan. This lady prefers to remain unknown, although where you're going the gods will know it any way!"

"You're going to kill me then?"

"Yes."

"And am I permitted to enquire 'why'?"

"Certainly. I am afraid that I shall be forced to kill you – though I regret it, sir, for I like you. You see, you have been enquiring just a little too pointedly to be harmless. I suspect that you are more than a common mercenary – that perhaps you are in the pay of Uffjir – and if this is so, then it will be more of a pleasure to kill you!"

"I am no Uffjirian, you oaf! And I am not involved in any intrigue. I seek my War Lord's son who disappeared some time ago! Think not that I would sink so low as you!"

The smile vanished from the Rhanian's face and his right hand clenched on his long sword.

"Then I am sorry! You see Nornos Rique is in this right up to his lance-tip!"

And with that, he raised his sword. The girl turned away, and just as Orfil was about to deal the death thrust, the door opened slowly and he saw the face of the Uffjirian nobleman. Behind him were half a dozen burly swordsmen.

"Yit take you, Parijh!" cried the spy and then to the girl, "Quick, get behind me and open the window. I'll hold them back. There are myats awaiting!"

And with that he rushed upon the Uffjirian who, for a moment was so taken aback that he could hardly defend himself from the furious attack of Orfil's sword.

"Quick men," he yelled, "seize him, kill him, don't let him escape!" But the narrow doorway would not permit more than one man to enter at a time and Orfil easily pushed Parijh back and swung the heavy bar into position as the door shut. back and swung the heavy bar into position as the door shut.

"No time to slay you now," he panted as he clambered over the window ledge, "perhaps some other time . . ."

The girl had by this time scrambled from the window and was waiting with the myats. The soft thud of their hooves was drowned by the yells of the man from Uffjir and the surly answers of his companions.

Silence fell as the men gave chase to Orfil and the girl. The mercenary still lay strapped to the bed. The door was barred from the inside and he had begun to think that he would soon starve to death when someone knocked on the door.

"*Get me out of here!*" he yelled.

"Is there anything the matter, sir?"

This was too much even for a hardened warrior. "Yes there is!" he roared, "and if you don't let me out right now – I'll tear the place down with my bare hands!" A rather vain boast considering his position.

Murmurs at the door and the retracing of steps down the creaking staircase.

He waited expectantly, hearing occasional voices. Then there were tramping feet on the stairway and in a few moments the door fell inwards, closely followed by two men with a battering log and behind them old Kerk.

"I *said* there was something up!" he exclaimed triumphantly.

It was a matter of minutes to untie the mercenary, for him to gather up his accoutrements, to pay Kerk and to find and saddle his myat. Then he was off, down the long forest track, following the trail of Orfil and his pursuers.

For three hours he followed a trail which was easily found. Once or twice he thought he heard movements in the forest but, although he kept his hand ever ready on his sword, he was not attacked.

Then, just as he turned the bend in the trail, they were there. The Uffjirian's men, lined across the narrow path, swords drawn and pikes at the ready.

But the mercenary was trained to quick thinking and at the same moment as his heels dug into his myat's flanks, he drew sword, unhooked shield and brought his lance to bear as he thundered down upon his foes, his crimson cloak flying behind him like a vampire's wings soaked in blood, and a blood-curdling war-shout on his lips!

Taken aback, they wavered, but at the Uffjirian's shouts behind them, pushed forward to meet the charging lancer. Down went one with a brilliantly tufted shaft protruding from his throat. The lance was wrenched out of the mercenary's hands and his steed reared and snorted, flailing with its cloven hooves. His face was alight with battle-lust, he ducked beneath the guard of another man and dealt him a cut which put him down, shrieking and calling to some unknown god in an agony of death. He whirled his steed about, hoping to gain a little ground by retreating, but it was too late, for he was surrounded by a solid ring of pikes and blue steel. He caught blow after blow on his shield and the flat of his sword. One man lunged upwards with his heavy pike and the myat snorted in pain before his deadly hooves beat the man down.

Leaping from the wounded myat, the lone swordsman found himself surrounded by four of Parijh's men. He bled from a dozen superficial cuts and still he fought with the skill and ferocity of a trained *crinja* cat. Then there was a gap in their ranks and he was through, rushing for a tethered myat 20 yards away.

Howling like were-wolves, they followed him across the glade and reached him just as he cut the tethering rope of the myat with his sword and leaped into the high saddle. They attempted to cut at his animal's legs but a swift arc of blue steel drove them back. As he passed the body of the man whom he had first slain, he stooped and wrenched the lance from the corpse and then he was away, down the long trail in the direction Orfil had taken. All his would-be captors heard was a grim laugh which echoed through the tall trees of the forest.

Turning in the saddle, the mercenary saw them run to their mounts and Parijh come from behind, scolding and cursing – for among other things, the fine beast the mercenary had taken had belonged to the Uffjirian!

And it soon proved its worth for he easily outdistanced them and was again following Orfil's tracks – a trail which was to lead to the weirdest adventure in his whole career.

THE SEA WOLVES!

Two days after his fight with the Uffjirian's men, the mercenary rode into the port of Minifjar in the country of Barj.

There were several ships in the harbour. Merchantmen mainly, but here and there rose the tall prows of warships.

Although their airships are motor-powered, the Zylorians have not found an engine capable of moving their ships, or for carrying them for very far and, since steam-power also is unknown, they still rely on sails and oars for motive power.

Most of the ships were equipped with both sails and oars but two of them were built for sails only. From every one of them, long barrels poked from strategic ports, for it was only a suicidal madman who would sail anything but the calm waters of the Asnogi Channel and the Shortani Sea unarmed.

There was one ship, a galley, which stood out from the others. Its tall prow triumphantly above the rest and its sails and paintwork were predominantly purple. Purple, like black on Earth, is the colour of death on Zylor, so it attracted much attention from the inhabitants of the small town.

The mercenary sought out the only presentable inn and bought a meal and a bed for the night.

As he lugged his equipment wearily up the flight of narrow stairs, he looked up and caught a glimpse of a familiar face – that of Orfil of Rhan's girl companion.

Evidently she had been watching him and the warrior kept a wary hand on his sword and resolved to make sure that his door was firmly barred that night.

But soon after he had dumped his belongings on the dirty bed, he heard the rattle of harness and, from his small window, he saw the spy and the girl leaving the walled entrance to the inn – they had none of their possessions with them which told the mercenary a great deal. They had gone for reinforcements. He sat on the edge of the bed pondering what he should do.

He had decided that it would be wiser to leave, when there came the sound of myat's hooves and a squad of Barjite Cavalry, fully armed with lances, swords, long rifles and pistols, clad in uniforms of blue, red and green with shining breastplates, helmets and leg greaves of bright steel. They clattered to a halt outside the inn.

"Thank Yit!" the mercenary murmured. For he recognised the captain of the mounted men as an old friend, who had fought beside him in an expedition Barj had made when bandits had been raiding their caravans of merchandise.

"Red!" he cried, opening the window. "Red, you son of a *crinja* cat!"

Red, or as his men knew him, Captain Jeodvir, Vollitt's son of Chathja, turned. Then, as he saw who called him, a wide grin took the place of his previously astonished expression and he passed a hand through the shock of hair which gave him his nickname.

'Sojan! What're you doing in this particular bit of Hell?"

"And you? One of King Vixian's crack lancers commanding a coast patrol?'

"The king doesn't like me any more, Sojan," laughed the warrior. "Not since I pressed for better pay for the cavalry and nearly started a civil war at the last council!"

It was Sojan's turn to laugh. "You couldn't plead for better conditions for the underpaid infantry, I suppose?"

"What? And have them get the idea that they're up to cavalry standard!"

The rivalry between infantry and mounted divisions in Barj was very real and at times became a threat to the internal peace of that nation. The brawls between the better trained cavalry (generally inheriting the right to become an officer) and the recruited infantry were cursed in every town from Erm to Ishtam-Zhem, the capital. But Sojan was not concerned with this, he had an ally now, no need to run, he could stay and fight like a man.

"Looking for a fight, Red?" he said.

"Dying to be killed, why?" enquired Red, using an expression which was currently popular among fighting men.

"Because I have a feeling that we will be in one soon!"

"Good, I'll tell my men to be prepared."

"Thanks, I'll need some help, I think."

"Unusual for you to admit *that*!"

"Shut up, I'm coming down."

In the courtyard of the inn, Sojan told Red what he knew about Orfil and what had happened to him since he left the court of Hatnor to search for his ruler's son.

And as he finished, Orfil and a band of some twenty mounted men in seamen's clothes, rode into the courtyard. The captain's squad consisted of ten men – so they were outnumbered almost two-to-one. The seamen had no lances but the cavalry had left their rifles, pistols and lances with their myats' saddles and other equipment. Now they were armed only with long sabres (or *vilthors*) and small battle-axes.

It took Orfil less than a second to take stock of the situation and with a curse, he bore down upon the group, yelling a blasphemous battle-shout so full of evil that it made Sojan's hair tingle. His men followed him, hardened sea-wolves these, all of them by rights fodder for the executioner's axe. Scarred, wild-eyed men in exotic clothes of many hues and nations. Black, green, white and red. From every nation on Zylor, they bore weapons which were equally varied – battle-axes, maces, pikes, hooked swords and broadswords, vilthors and blades resembling scimitars. All were there, and many so strange that they defied simple description.

Sojan blocked Orfil's lance thrust with his own long sword and unslung his shield from his back in a hurry. But not soon enough, for Orfil's lance stabbed again and flung the mercenary backward against a wall. Luckily, the lance tip broke on Sojan's breastplate and Orfil swore to his dark gods as he wheeled his steed about and attempted to cut at Sojan with his broadsword. But now Sojan was up again, back against the wall, shield up and blade screaming as he cut past Orfil's guard.

But Orfil was swept away as the fight eddied back and forth across the courtyard. There, a green man of Poltoon went down with a lancer on top of him, stabbing again and again. Near him a huge red man, bearded, with one of his small horns broken and splintered, staggered towards his tethered steed spitting blood from a punctured lung – he never made the myat. A lancer was crushed by sheer weight of numbers as four howling, long-haired black men from Shortani bore him down and almost tore him to pieces. Everywhere was chaos and Sojan hardly knew who it was he fought, there were so many of them. Finally he singled out another red giant who whirled a shrieking twin-bladed axe around his head and laughed through his black beard all the time. He bled from a flesh wound in his left arm and his face streamed blood from a superficial sword cut, but he never seemed to tire. Sojan caught a blow of the axe on his shield which dented so much that it almost broke his arm. Discarding it he skipped nimbly away from the arc of blood-stained steel, ducked beneath it and ripped upwards with a thrust that caught the giant in the throat and threw him groaning to the cobbles before Sojan lost sight of him as a fresh wave of sea-spoilers pushed towards him.

The war-shout of his people was upon Sojan's lips and it rose above the screams and curses of the men, spurred Red and his men on to greater feats of magnificent swordsmanship until the sailors were driven back. Slowly, very slowly, they gave ground and just as victory seemed in the hands of Sojan and his allies, from the courtyard walls dropped scores of well-armoured axemen.

It was impossible to defend themselves against this sudden onslaught and the last thing Sojan heard as an axe haft fell on his helmet and blackness followed blinding light was:

"Take them alive. They will suffer more tonight!"

SOJAN AT SEA

Sojan awoke with a piercing pain in his head which quickly disappeared. Looking about him, he found that he was lying on a comfortable couch in a well furnished room which seemed to have an indefinable 'something' wrong with it.

Then he realised what it was. Every article of furniture was clamped to the floor and the windows were small square openings in the walls, just below eye-level.

He was in a ship's cabin! Obviously one of the ships in the harbour – that was why the men who had attacked him had worn seafaring garb. Which ship though? He didn't know. Doubtless he would find out soon enough. Could it be the purple ship of death which swayed at anchor in Minifjar harbour? It was likely, this business was mysterious enough for anything.

He walked over to the port hole and looked out. No, the purple ship could be seen from there. Then what ship was this?

He went back to the couch after trying the door which he found locked as he had expected.

He waited an hour – a long hour – until the bar on the door was lifted with a creak and the door swung open.

To his surprise, he found himself staring into the face of Parijh, the Uffjirian who said:

"Welcome aboard the *Sea Crinja* my friend!"

But the man who stood behind Parijh caught the adventurer's attention most of all. It was his War Lord's son, Nornos Rique of Hatnor!

"Shiltain!" swore Sojan when he saw him. "What – ?"

"Explanation later, Sojan, we were lucky to rescue you. Right now you're not very welcome. My fault, I suppose, for giving no hint that I would be going – but there was no time."

"But how did I get out of Orfil's hands?"

"It's a long story – too long to relate here. Meanwhile, we sail for the Sea of Demons!"

"What?"

"We're sailing dangerous waters Sojan, for we play a dangerous game in which the whole planet is the stake. Do you want to come on deck?"

"Thanks."

The three men climbed the long ladders to the poopdeck. Nornos Rique shouted orders as sails were set and men moved to their oars. All the men were well built fighting men.

Sojan looked back to where the huge purple galley swayed at anchor like a dead ship becalmed in the terrible weed jungle of the Black Ocean. She gave no signs of following and soon the sails were billowing, oars creaked in unison and they were on the open sea, bound for the mysterious Sea of Demons.

Like all ships, there was continual movement aboard. Men scurrying up and down the rigging, guns oiled and cleaned, the shouts of the mate giving orders.

The ship comprised three decks. Two raised fore and aft and a middle deck which was little more than a raised platform over the oarsmen's pits on port and starboard. In the centre of this deck there was another slightly raised platform measuring about thirty feet upon which was the single mast. At the base of this mast a drummer sat – beating out a steady rhythm which was followed by the oars who took their timing from the drum.

On this platform, also, was the heavy artillery and something which Sojan had never seen before – harpoon guns, twelve of them, five a side and another two fore and aft.

It was obvious that peaceful trading with the tribes along the Shortani coast was not the object of this particular voyage.

Suddenly, Sojan remembered his comrades.

"What happened to my friends?" he asked.

"They're all aboard the *Purple Arrow*, that cursed ship of Death you saw in Minifjar harbour," answered Rique. "You see, Sojan, we only had time to free you before we were discovered. My men and I swam across and boarded her silently last night. We finally found you and, judging by your snores, you were in a drugged sleep. There were four others with you but they were so much dead weight that we could only take you and secretly leave knives in their shirts with which to aid themselves if they have the chance. I'm sorry, Sojan, but it is too late to go back for them now even if it were practical."

"You are right, of course, Rique," answered Sojan, "but I would that I could help them!"

Now the tall *Sea Crinja* was in open waters, beyond sight of land. Bound for the terrible Sea of Demons where few ships ever sailed – and returned. And, in the days they sailed towards their destination, Sojan pieced together the ominous tale of the Old Ones and how the Priests of Rhan sought to conquer Zylor with their evil aid.

It seemed that word of the plot was brought to Uffjir first. This country lies due North of Rhan on the Shortani coast and is generally better informed about the Island of Mystery as it is sometimes called than is the rest of Zylor.

The Uffjirian monarch, King Ashniophil, had feared to make public the news as it would very likely force the Rhanian priesthood into swifter action. Instead, he had sent a messenger to enlist Nornos Rique's aid as, if the worst ever happened, Hatnor was the most powerful country on the whole planet. Nornos Rique, naturally, had not thought it wise to notify his father at once as he knew the other's aptitude to make quick, but sometimes hasty decisions and this is what Uffjir was trying to prevent.

Unfortunately, at the time of the messenger's coming, the Princess Asderma had been with Rique and had overheard everything. She threatened to betray Nornos Rique to the Rhanians unless he paid her a fabulous amount of money.

Knowing that even when she had the money, she would be dangerous, Rique decided to go into hiding. He had had to kidnap the girl and ride for Rhan in an effort to come to terms with the rulers or, if this failed, destroy or capture their leaders and their strange unhuman allies.

After several detours, he finally reached Minifjar but not before the Princess had escaped and fled to Orfil who had promptly ridden for Minifjar himself where a ship (one of the purple fleet of the Rhanian Theocracy – or Priest Rulers) awaited him in case just such an emergency as this should occur. The mercenary's questions had aroused his interest when he had overheard them at the inn and he had taken Sojan prisoner. Only to be foiled by the Uffjirian messenger who was acting as a rear-guard for Nornos Rique. The rest Sojan knew.

Now it was a race to get to Rhan first.

THE SEA OF DEMONS

It was a race to get to Rhan first. The *Purple Arrow* would take the comparatively safe way there by sailing down the coast of Poltoon until safer waters were reached (namely the Poltoonian Ocean) and back to Rhan via these waters.

The *Crinja*, however, would attempt to sail through the Demon Sea, cutting off a considerable part of the distance. They knew little of what they had to fight against. The *Arrow* did not know of their plan and was relying on the greater speed to catch the *Crinja* and either destroy it or beat it to Rhan and have it destroyed then. If the *Crinja* could reach Rhan first, it would have several days start and the fate of the world would be decided in those days. Why the *Arrow* had not sailed earlier, they knew not, but guessed that they were waiting for someone.

It was a day's sail until they would reach the Demon Sea and in that time, Sojan got to know his companions better.

Parijh, the Uffjirian, proved to be a humorous man. Cheerful in the face of every danger they had had to meet. When necessary, he was an excellent swordsman but preferred to keep out of what he called 'unnecessary brawling'. This often gained him a reputation of cowardliness but, as he said, it was an asset rather than otherwise, for what better opponent is there than the one who underestimates you?

Sojan had to agree with this statement and a strong feeling

of comradeship and mutual respect grew between them as they sailed ever nearer to the Sea of Demons.

Nornos Rique himself captained the *Crinja*. Rique was a tall man with a face that, though not handsome, had a dependable and rock-hard ruggedness and eyes of steel grey.

The mate was, as is usual on Zylorian naval craft, either privateer or part of an authorised Navy, a cavalry captain by the name of Andel of Riss who, although inclined to make independent decisions without consulting anyone first, was a good man in any kind of fight, and worth four of any man in the crew, who were all fine men and who admired him and respected him as only seamen can respect a man. They would also prove this in a fight with man or the elements.

The custom of placing cavalry men as seconds-in-command of ships is not as strange as it seems and the custom evolved thus :

At one time in the not-so-ancient history of Zylor a strong rivalry developed between seamen and landsmen. It became so bad that if a war came, the land forces could never rely on the naval forces – and vice versa.

It was the idea of assigning landsmen to learn the ways of the sea and naval officers to get to know the cavalry and infantry that saved them from chaos, and nowadays the two forces worked together in perfect harmony.

Later, on the evening of the third day out of Minifjar they were sailing a sea which was similar to any other sea but which, according to the maps, was the feared Sea of Demons.

"We'd better anchor here and sail on at daybreak," Nornos Rique decided, and he gave the order to drop anchor. The anchor chain rattled down for several minutes before stopping with a jarring clank.

"Water's too deep, sir ! Anchor won't take !" yelled Andel.

"Then we daren't drift. Ship oars and set sail on your course."

"Yes, sir !"

Night fell forming an atmosphere of decay and death which could almost be smelled or touched. But apart from this, nothing happened save a faint scraping from time to time along the side of the boat which was attributed to some heavy sea-weed or a piece of drift wood.

The twin suns rose and the green dawn came, sending shadows and atmosphere scurrying over the horizon. The sea was green and shone like dark jade with some of jade's intangible mistiness.

Oars smashed into it, ploughing it in bright foam-flecked furrows, and the monotonous beat of the drum began.

Sojan and his comrades ate breakfast in an atmosphere of gloom.

"It's this confounded sea!" suddenly roared Andel, rising from his chair and crashing his fist into his open palm. "Yit! By the time this voyage is over, there'll be men's lives lost and most likely we'll all be on the bottom!"

"Calm down, Andel, we'll come to any danger when we get to it," Nornos Rique said.

Andel grunted sullenly and subsided.

Two depressed hours followed until :

"Yit take us!"

This oath was followed by a piercing scream which tailed off into a choking gasp.

The four men rushed on deck. Most of the crew were at the starboard rail, staring downwards to where a red foam flecked the white.

"Turn back, sir, you must turn back!" One hysterical seaman rushed towards Nornos Rique screaming.

"Calm down, and tell me what happened!"

Fear was in the man's eyes. A terrible fear bordering on madness. He babbled out his tale.

"A – a *thing*, – sir – it crept up on Mitesh and – oh, sir – it grabbed him by the throat and jumped overboard!"

"Is that all?"

"It's enough, sir!" murmured another of the men.

"What did this 'thing' look like? Who saw it clearly?"

"I did, sir."

It was the man who had commented a second before.

"Well?"

"It was a kind of green and brown. Scaly. By Yit, sir, it looked like a man might look if his mother had been a fish!"

"You mean this animal was – human?"

"Not *human*, sir. But it had a man's body sure enough. And his face was pointed, like, sir. And his *eyes* – his eyes were green, like the rest of him, and seemed to rot you when he stared at you!"

"All right. Thank you. Take this man below and give him something to drink!"

"Yes sir. Do we turn back?"

"No! You all knew there was danger!"

"Danger, yes sir, but not from – from *devils*!"

"Get below – we sail on!"

Back in their cabin, Sojan spoke.

"I've heard old folktales, Rique, about occurrences such as this one. Now I know why the ancients called this the 'Sea of Demons'."

"Do you think they are – organised in any way?"

"I've never heard of them being anything *but* in large numbers!"

"Perhaps this was a warning, then?"

"I think it might have been."

"We'd better set all guns in readiness. Those harpoons will come in useful. I had them mounted in case of meeting any of those large saurians that inhabit the Poltoonian Ocean. But it looks as if they'll be needed for a different 'game' now!"

The ship's oars began to creak again. But was the beat of the drum less sure? Were the oars a heartbeat slower? It seemed to the men standing on the poop deck that this was so.

Towards the middle of the day, the atmosphere of death grew and suddenly from the sea on four sides of the vessel the weird inhabitants of the Sea of Demons rose and attempted to board them.

But this time they were ready and the guns sent forth a steady stream of deadly missiles, driving the shrieking horde back into the sea.

"They went quickly enough!" yelled Andel jubilantly.

"Too quickly. They'll be more wary next time and they'll be back at night for sure!"

And night did fall and with it strange sounds which rose from the water and chilled the blood of the men on board.

But this time the crew were prepared and their searchlights stabbed the gloom, picking out the grotesque figures of the sea people.

The crew moved forward, their yells mingling with the strange hissing cries of the sea people. Sabres flashed in the searchlight glare and the blood of seamen and the man-like monsters mingled on the deck, making it difficult to get a footing.

The ship was a contrast of glaring light and total blackness. Men leaped from shadow into blinding gleam or disappeared into murky darkness. Men's breath was steaming in the cold night air. Men's battle cries pierced the shadows where light failed. And Sojan and his companions were in the thick of it, their swords lashing this way and that at their inhuman adversaries. Sojan's war-cry spurred on the men and slowly, then swiftly, they pushed them back and the body of the last monster to invade their ship crashed over the rail to splash into the murky waters below.

There was an audible sigh from the sweating men.

"We've pushed 'em back once, lads, and by Yit, we'll push them back from here to Rhan if needs be!" cried Sojan. With the thrill of victory still in their hearts, their pulses tingling with conquest, the men's voices rose in assent.

A brief count found two sailors suffering from wounds where the talons of the sea-people had ripped them, while three more men were missing, obviously dragged down by the sea-people.

"We should reach Rhan in a day," said Nornos Rique.

"Or the bottom," broke in Andel gloomily.

But the monotonous day ahead was broken only by the screaming of sea-birds as they passed the outlying islands of The Immortal Theocracy of Rhan as it was called. This 'immortal theocracy' was little more than Rhan itself and a group of four islands inhabited mainly by primitive tribes, most of whom dwelt in the interior, anyway, and had probably never heard of Rhan.

As they neared Rhan, Sojan felt misgivings. Would they succeed in carrying out their plan? Or would their perilous journey be in vain.

It was with these odd questions in his mind that he followed his friends down the gangplank and down a series of narrow lanes to a private house owned by a society known to those few holding positions of trust in the Hatnorian Empire, as the 'Friends of Hatnor'. These 'friends' were generally native Hatnorians carrying forged or, as in some cases, real papers giving assumed names as well as assumed nationalities.

Three long knocks and two short ones three times repeated gained them admission.

As they walked along the narrow corridor to the main living room they began to feel just a little more secure, even though they were deep in the heart of the enemy's city – Jhambeelo.

But as the door swung open and friendly light flooded into the dark corridor they were taken aback!

"Hello, Sojan," grinned Red. "I don't think I've met your friends?"

"By Yit! Red, how did you get here before us?" cried Sojan.

"Simple. I flew!"

"What? No airship could make the distance."

'You're quite right. I didn't come by airship. Banjar, here, brought me!"

For the first time the comrades noticed what appeared to be a hunchbacked, rather tall, man with piercing blue eyes and aquiline features. Dark-haired, with a swarthy complexion.

"To snap the bow in half," said Red, using a term common on Zylor which means roughly – 'To cut a long story short', "Jik, Wanwif, Selwoon and myself succeeded in staving a rather large hole in the bottom of the *Purple Arrow*. Naturally enough, it was not long before we were beginning to regret this as the water was rising steadily in the hold. Then, as we were all good swimmers, I thought that the only way to escape drowning would be to enlarge the hole and get out that way. So in turns we widened the hole and, with a great deal of difficulty, pulled ourselves under the keel of the boat and up into the open water. We lost Wanwif, I'm sorry to say. He didn't make it. Well, after that we found that we would have been better off drowning in the ship as there was no sight of land. I learned afterwards that we were in the Black Ocean and this didn't help as the stories I've heard of the Black Ocean are anything but cheerful. But believe it or not, after swimming in a Westerly direction for an hour or so, we were picked up by a little fishing vessel, oared only, manned by some natives of Yoomik which is the largest of the Rhanian group next to Rhan itself.

"The people looked after us but soon we got weary of hanging around their village and decided that an exploratory trip into the interior of the island would be the only thing to break the monotony. We trekked for several days until coming upon the village of Banjar's people – the Ascri.

"The Ascri at one time were enslaved by the Rhanian Priesthood and still bear a grievance against them. It was Banjar who, when he had heard that I believed you were going to Rhan, suggested that he fly me there. We landed at night and made our way here. Banjar's people are advanced in many of the crafts and sciences and they have an asset which helps them tremendously. Show Sojan and his friends your asset, Bonjar!"

Bonjar grinned and stood up. Unfolding a pair of huge wings.

"My people, I believe, are descended from the ancient winged mammals who used to live on Zylor. Just an off-shoot of evolution, I suppose. But one which has proved of great help to my people who can travel great distances at great speeds and although we are few in number, we can elude any enemies by leaving the ground and escaping that way. As my friend says, 'It is a great asset'!"

Formal introductions were made and food eaten but when this was finished Sojan spoke to Red.

"Have you managed to find out anything which might prove useful to us, Red?"

"I have indeed, my friend, I have found out something which, with your courage and skill and a great deal of luck, will save the world from chaos!"

PRISONERS IN STONE

Red's plan was simple enough. Members of the secret society of the 'Friends of Hatnor' had found an ancient plan of the Great Temple which was both chief place of worship and the centre of the Priesthood's rule in Rhan. There were three tunnels leading into it. Old sewers, long since disused. Two were cul-de-sacs, having been walled up. But in the last, the walling had been a hasty job and the bricks used to seal it had collapsed. However, these tunnels were still guarded at the other end. Some said by Palace Guards – but others said simply that they were guarded by 'something'. Even if the foe was human it would take an incredibly brave man to venture the rotting tunnels.

"Why not an army?" asked Andel. "Surely a great many men would be safer than one?"

"Safer, yes, but certainly not so secret. Every action we make must not be detected by the Priesthood – otherwise we are lost. We can only make a very wide guess at what power these Old Ones wield and it is our aim to stop them using it – not bring it down upon our heads – and the rest of the world's heads, also."

"I see," said Parijh, "then let me be the one to go. I offer not out of heroics – which are extremely bad taste in any case – but I am more accustomed to stealth than these sword-swinging barbarians with me." He grinned.

J·CAWTHORN·76

"Ho! So that's what we are, are we?" roared Andel. "I'll have you know . . ."

But the comrades would never hear the rest of Andel's forthcoming witticism for Red broke in: "Be a bit quieter, Andel, or you'll have the whole of the Rhanian Soldiery on our heads!"

"Sorry," said Andel.

"No," continued Red, "I think Sojan should go. He is better for the job than anyone else. He has barbarian training, he is cat-footed, lynx-eyed and can hear a sword sing in its scabbard a mile away. I think he will succeed in getting through more than any other man in our company!"

"Then it will be I, that's settled," said Sojan with satisfaction. "When and where do I start?"

"You start now, and I will lead you to the entrance of the tunnel. I suggest that you take a rifle, an axe, your shield and your long sword. Half-armour would be advisable, also."

"Then I shall take your advice," Sojan laughed and proceeded to don half-armour. This consisted of greaves for his legs, and a breastplate and helmet.

Then he was ready and prepared to follow Red down winding backstreets to a small turning near the Great Temple. Here, Red lifted a rusted cover to reveal an equally rusted ladder leading down into darkness.

"Good luck!" was all he said as Sojan slipped down into the gloom and sought about for hand- and foot-holds on the age-worn rail. Then the lid was replaced and Sojan found himself in utter darkness.

Down he fumbled, sometimes missing footing where one of the metal bars had rusted away, once nearly falling when his groping hand instead of closing on solid metal closed on damp air. But at last he was on the uneven floor of the disused sewer, peering into the gloom. He followed the wall along for what seemed an eon, stumbling over fallen bricks and refuse. At last he sensed an obstruction ahead and he unsheathed his sword and felt the reassuring butt of his heavy pistol in his hand. On he went, past the fallen wall until – suddenly – there was no more tunnel. Or so it seemed. His right hand, which had been groping along the wall touched nothing. But after the first brief shock he grinned to himself. This was the right hand turn of the tunnel. Soon he would meet the Guardians.

And meet them he did for, with a soul-shaking shriek, two of the mysterious guardians were upon him. Huge reptilian things, red-eyed and red-mouthed with teeth reaching a foot long and razor sharp.

Sojan, shocked by their sudden attack, took a step backwards, hitched his rifle to his shoulder and fired straight into the mouth of the foremost beast. It shrieked again but still came on. Hastily he dropped the rifle and replaced it with his heavy axe and long sword. But before the beast reached him it had stumbled and fallen with crumpling forelegs, writhing in a fit of agony which ended with one abrupt shudder of death.

The other monster was checked for a moment, sniffed the corpse of its companion and then voiced another spine-chilling shriek which was half hiss and half human cry. Sojan met it with sword lashing and axe whining through the air about his head. Back went the monster but it returned in an instant, clutching at Sojan with its claws which almost resembled human hands – though hands with six inch steel talons on the ends of each finger. Sojan stumbled backwards, his axe cutting and hacking at the hideous thing, his sword slashing into its throat again and again until at last it was down in a death agony that lasted minutes.

Pausing to wipe his weapons clean of blood and to pick up his rifle, Sojan moved on down the tunnel, feeling a little more cheerful now that he knew his foe and had conquered it.

And, abruptly, he was at the end of the tunnel and a similar steel ladder, in better condition, leading upwards. Warily he clambered up. Rifle, axe and shield strapped across his broad back and his sword firmly clenched in his teeth.

There was a metal cover here, too, and he lifted it cautiously to be blinded for a moment by the sudden gleam. He had been so long in darkness and the semi-darkness of the tunnel that he blinked hard for several seconds until his eyes became accustomed to the light.

Silently he eased his body through the narrow hole and just as softly replaced the cover. He was in a lighted corridor with torches on either side. The corridor was short and had a door at each end. Which door? He decided immediately to take the door which led farthest away from the tunnel. At least he would be a little deeper into the Temple and nearer the Inner Room in the centre which housed the Old Ones.

Gradually he pushed the door until it swung open. He thanked the Gods of Light, Yit and Corrunj, that they had not been locked.

Down another corridor he sped, cat-footed as ever, wary hands on sword and rifle. His armour glinted in the torch-light and his shadow loomed black and huge on the wall.

Most of the priests would be at rest, he knew, but it was equally certain that guards would be posted at strategic points and absolute caution was necessary. He had a rough plan of the Temple printed in his mind but the maze of corridors which he was following and which ran deeper and deeper into the heart of the Temple were complicated and were probably of more recent origin for the map had been very old.

But cautious as he knew he must be he was certainly not slow. For every heartbeat counted. He had to reach the chamber of the Old Ones somehow and discover who – or what – they were and what their motives were for allying themselves with the evil Priesthood of Rhan.

The murmurs of voices. The laughs of men. The clank of sword-scabbard against armour. At last, a guarded entrance. Was he near the strange sanctuary of the Old Ones?

The men's backs were to him. This was not the time for heroics, for a cry would mean discovery; and discovery he must avoid. He raised his rifle and brought it down on the head of one guard while with his other hand he chopped at the back of the other man's neck. They both collapsed without a murmur. Looking up and down the intersecting corridor to make sure he had not been seen, he grabbed the two bodies by their loose clothing and pulled them back into the shadows. No time to hide them. And no time to hide himself. For the clank of steel-shod feet resounded down the corridor. He hugged the wall and prayed to his ancient gods that he would not be discovered.

Sojan heard the steps come nearer and nearer, and then, miraculously, fade away again. Risking discovery, he peered round the wall and saw another passage-way. Down it strode two guards and one of the infamous High Priests of Rhan, the rulers of the place. Cat-footed as usual, he followed them. This corridor was not very well lighted but, unlike the others, it had doors set in the walls.

Sojan hoped that one of these would not open.

Suddenly the priest stopped.

"Wait here," Sojan heard him say. No time to think, now, he must act. Into the nearest apartment and pray to Yit that it was unoccupied.

Luck! The rooms were empty. These, Sojan could see, were the apartments of the High Priests. No monkish sparsity of furniture here – these rooms were lavishly furnished and decorated. Grinning, Sojan bounced down on to the bed and breathed a prayer of relief. Then he was up again and taking in his surroundings. On one wall hung several of the long flowing robes which the High Priests wore.

One of the customs of these men was to go veiled – to give them a little more security from the assassin, Sojan guessed – and also to enable them to slip from the Temple and mingle with the people without fear of being recognised. This was one of the reasons why the people of Rhan were so easily kept in subjection by the evil Priest-Rulers.

But there was a chance, though Sojan knew it was a slim one, that he could don one of these robes and enter the Inner Chamber and meet the mysterious Old Ones face to face.

Quickly he slipped into the robe, stuffing all but his sword and pistol under a nearby couch and hoping that they would not be discovered. His sword and pistol were well hidden by the folds of the robe and he could keep his armour on.

Out now, and down the passage, past the lounging soldiers who sprang to attention and saluted him with the usual Zylorian salute – clenched fists against temples and a short bow from the waist.

Sojan acknowledged the salute by a curt nod of his head. The veil hid his features entirely, and if he was unmasked by some mishap – only the other High Priests would know whether he was a fraud or not. So, comparatively safe, Sojan moved along the corridor towards the huge, metal-studded door which was the portal to the Inner Chamber.

It was unlocked, and the guards on each side of it stood away respectfully as Sojan opened it.

At first he could see nothing, the room was lit by one torch which cast shadows everywhere. Then, from one corner of the large chamber, a voice spoke. It was a voice of infinite weariness, full of lost hope and the knowledge of an eternity of despair.

"Why trouble us again, Priest, we have promised to do your bidding? And *we* keep our word – if you do not."

Sojan realised that instead of the evil forces he had expected, here were prisoners; slaves rather than allies of the Priesthood.

"I'm no priest," he said, "if I knew who you were I might help you even!"

"Is this another trick, Priest," murmured the voice, although this time there was a little hope in it.

"No trick. I'm a sworn enemy of the priesthood of Rhan. I represent the rest of Zylor, who have no wish to become enslaved by the Rhanians. Yet rumour has it that you are allied with them." He squinted into the darkness, "Who are you – or what?"

"We are the old inhabitants of Zylor. We lived here before ever the shining ships of humanity sprang from distant planets in a desperate attempt to reach another habitable planet. They thought that the end of their world had come. As it happened their world did not die, but it was too late then, they had taken all their knowledge out into space with them, and in the long journey from Galaxy to Galaxy much of their knowledge perished, for the journey took centuries to complete.

"By the time the new generations reached this planet, their ancestors had died and Man had to start again, almost from the beginning. These Men, who called themselves 'Lemurians' lived peacefully with us for many hundreds of years and we helped them as much as possible, for we are a very ancient race and had more knowledge than ever the ancestors of the Lemurians, although of a different kind – for while Man concentrated on improving his body, we concentrated on improving our minds and could control mighty elements with our wills. Eventually the Men became frightened of us and sent us away (there were only a few of us living in far-flung colonies then; now we are even less)."

"But how did you become the slaves of these priests?" asked Sojan. "What happened?"

"Although there were many men who feared us and called us Things of Evil and similar names, there were others who began to worship us for our powers, calling us Gods and setting up altars and Temples to us.

"Just as some men are foolish, some of our number were foolish and began to think that perhaps they *were* Gods after all. They dwelt in the Temples and had sacrifices made to them and took part in meaningless rituals. The priests soon found their weaknesses, however, and decided that they could rule the people if they frightened them by telling them of the wrath of the gods and so on. They succeeded in capturing us and imprisoning us. I was one of the foolish ones, our contemporaries have long since left this planet in search of another, uninhabited by Man, with whom they cannot live in peace.

"You may have read in your history scrolls of the mighty Theocracy which dominated the world at one time. Rhan is now all that is left of the Theocracy – a remnant of a great and terrible nation! The people rose against their oppressors, country by country, until the evil Priesthood was driven back, further and further, to seek refuge on this island, the original capital of the old Imperial Theocracy. It was here that the cult, based on worship of us, was spawned and, if you can help us, it is here that it will die. Otherwise a new Black Age shall cover the world in a cloak of death!"

"But," cried Sojan, "if you do not wish them to rule Man then why do you help them? Why do you lend them your powers to destroy the great Nations of Zylor?"

"They have promised us freedom, O, Man! Freedom after thousands of decades. Freedom after eons of despair. We would follow our brothers, we would travel the infinite lengths of Space and Time were we once released. We would see Suns and Planets, green things. Seas and Plains. For us these things are worth more than life. We are *of* them more than Man – for we, like the planets and the stars, and the grass that grows for ever, are almost immortal. We have no bodies, as Man knows bodies, no senses as Man interprets senses – we are Minds. You can see that the temptation is great! We were not strong-willed to begin with, we were proud of Man's petty ceremonies. Now that he offers us Light and Freedom again, we *must* accept. Unless there is another way."

"There may be another way," Sojan said. "If you will but tell me *how* you are imprisoned, perhaps I can release you!'

"There are certain minerals, rare and almost unknown, which have the properties that lead has compared to radium. Radium cannot harm or pass through lead. Similarly, although we can pass through most minerals and life forms, we are imprisoned if we enter a certain precious stone. We can enter it, but by some strange trick of nature, our beings cannot pass back through it. Thus we were enticed, centuries ago, into these blocks of *ermtri* stone. The only way in which we can escape is by someone outside boring shafts into the blocks and thus cutting channels through which we can pass.

"Do you understand?"

Dimly Sojan understood, though his brain was shaken by the effort of trying to imagine beings so utterly alien to Man, yet in some ways akin to him. He picked up the torch and cast its light towards the centre of the hall. There on an altar, covered by a crimson cloth, rested five large blocks of some dark, cloudy blue substance. Like – like blue jade. It was a stone that Sojan, who had travelled the whole of his planet almost, had never seen – had never, what is more, heard of – not even in legends.

"I understand," he said, "what tool will cut it?"

"Steel, sharp steel will bore into it. Have you steel?"

"Yes. Will it hurt you?"

"No, it will leave no impression."

Wiping sweat from his forehead and hands, Sojan moved towards the blocks. He drew his sword and clambered up on to the altar. Placing the sharp point of his blade on top of the first block, he turned it round and round. Feeling it bite deeper and deeper into the strange substance he became aware of a strange tingling which seemed to flow up his sword and into his body, he couldn't define it but it was not unpleasant. Suddenly there was a dazzling burst of green and orange brightness and something seemed to flow from the hole that he had bored, flow out and upwards, lighting the room. He heard no words, but in his mind there was a great sense of joy – of thanks. Then, one by one he saw the other blocks, broken by the same strange power, open and the green and orange brightness flow from them.

Then they took on a slightly more solid shape, until Sojan could make out eyes and circular bodies. These, then, were the Old Ones. Perhaps in a million, million years, man too would have succeeded in being able to form the atoms of his body into whatever shape he desired. Perhaps, these beings once were Men? That would explain the strange kinship Sojan felt for them. A kinship which his Lemurian ancestors felt also, before their witnessing of such alien powers changed their finer feelings into those of fear and hate.

"Before you leave," Sojan begged, "I crave one request as a price for your release."

"Anything!"

"Then when I am out this building and safely at sea, destroy this place of Evil so that the power of the priests will be shattered for all time and such an evil can never rise again!"

"Gladly we grant you this. We will wait here until you are at sea. But tread carefully, we cannot help you to escape."

Thanking them, Sojan turned about and left, sword in hand. But in his exultation he had forgotten the soldiers outside and they stared in amazement at the sword in his hand and the sweat on his face. This did not seem to them any High Priest.

Taking quick stock of the situation, Sojan spoke to them.

"I – I had a little difficulty with one of the bolts on the interior," he lied, "I had to use this sword to loosen it . . ."

With a puzzled look, the men bowed and saluted, but there was doubt in their eyes.

"A priest would not go unveiled for anything," he heard one of them murmur as he entered the room which he had left previously. "He doesn't seem a priest to me! Here you, stop a minute!"

But Sojan had bolted the door and was hastily donning his weapons again. The men began to bang on the door and more men came to see what the noise was about.

"That's no priest," he heard someone say, "The High Priest Thoro is conducting the Ceremony of Death in the Outer Temple! He won't be back for hours!"

"Batter the door down you fools," came a voice that was obviously that of one in authority, probably a High Priest.

Anxiously, Sojan looked for another exit. There was only a curtained window.

He parted the curtain, and looked outside. It was still dark. He looked down. A courtyard scarcely ten feet below. *With luck*, he thought, *I can jump down there and escape as best I can*. He put a foot on the ledge and swung himself over, dropping lightly to the grass of the courtyard. In the centre of the courtyard a fountain splashed quietly – a scene of peace and solitude. But not for long. He saw a face at the window he had so recently quit.

"He's down there," one of the soldiers shouted.

Sojan ducked into the nearest doorway, opposite the room he had left. He ran down a short, dark corridor and up a flight of steps. No sign of pursuit yet. Panting heavily he ran in the direction he knew an exit to be. It would be guarded now, he knew, for the whole Temple was by this time alert. And so it was. With his usual good luck, Sojan had succeeded in making the exit unchallenged. But there would be no such luck here, with five huge soldiers coming at him.

Again he had no time for heroics. His pistol came up and two of his would-be killers went down. The other three were on him now and his sword cut a gleaming arc about his head. His battle-axe shrieked as if for blood as he carried the attack towards his foes instead of they to him. Nonplussed for a second, they fell back.

That falling back was for them death, for now Sojan had some kind of advantage and he made full use of it as he drove blow after blow, thrust after thrust into the men.

Bleeding himself from several wounds, Sojan came on, down went one man, then another. Now the last warrior, fighting with desperation hacked and parried, and sought an opening in Sojan's amazing guard.

None came, the man sought an opening too often, lunged forward – and almost pinioned himself on Sojan's blade. Back he tried to leap, clumsily. A perfect target for a whistling, battered axe to bury itself in helmet and brain.

Leaving his axe where it had come to rest, Sojan fled the Temple. His heart pounding, he finally reached the house where his friends waited.

"Come," he cried, "I'm successful – but we must make the ship immediately, all of us, else we all die. I don't know what they intend to do."

His companions realised that there was no time for an explanation and followed him wordlessly.

A frantic race for the docks. One brief skirmish with a City Patrol and then they were on board. Up anchor, out oars, cast-off.

And as the ship sped from the harbour they looked back.

There came a blinding flash and then a deep, rolling roar as the great temple erupted in a sudden burst of flame. Then, as they peered back at the city, there was blackness again. The temple was not burning – there was no temple now to burn – it had been dissolved.

As they watched, Sojan and his friends saw five streaks of blue and orange flame rise skyward and rocket upwards and outwards – towards the stars.

"What was that?" gasped Nornos Rique.

"The Old Ones," smiled Sojan. "I'll tell you a tale which you may not believe. But it is a tale which has taught me much – as well as giving me a valuable history lesson!"

The voyage back was not a boring one for Sojan's companions as they listened to his strange tale.

But what of the Purple Galley you ask, what of Orfil and the Princess who betrayed Rique? That, readers, is a story which is short and sad. They, too, attempted to sail through the Sea of Demons in pursuit of Sojan and his companions.

But they were not so lucky.

SOJAN AND THE PLAIN OF MYSTERY

(1958)

The wind tore at the rigging of the tiny air-cruiser as it pushed bravely into the howling storm.

Four men clung to the deck rails whilst a fifth strove to steer the tossing gondola.

"Keep her headed North!" yelled Nornos Rique to Sojan.

"At this rate we'll be tossed on to Shortani unless the wind shifts!" he yelled back.

Parijh, the Shortanian grimaced.

"I've been meaning to go home for some time!" he called.

"You'll be home for your own funeral unless someone gives me a hand with this wheel!" cried Sojan.

Sojan, Nornos Rique, Parijh, Andel and Red, the five men who had saved their planet of Zylor from the evil priest-rulers of Rhan some months ago, were returning to Hatnor after being the guests of honour at several banquets held to celebrate their triumph. Sojan, Rique, Andel and Red had been uncomfortable about the whole thing, only Parijh, always glad of the limelight, had enjoyed himself thoroughly.

The storm had sprung up quickly and they were now battling to keep the little dirigible into the wind which drove them steadily southwards.

"Wouldn't it be better to land, Sojan?" Andel shouted.

"It would be, my friend, if we knew where we were. There's every likelihood of getting out of this trouble into something worse."

Suddenly there was a loud snapping sound and the wheel spun throwing Sojan off balance and on to the deck.

"What was that?" yelled Parijh.

"Steering's gone! We can't attempt to repair it in this weather. We'll just have to drift now!"

The five trooped down into the tiny cabin. Even there it was not warm and they were all depressed as they shivered in their cloaks and attempted to get some sleep.

Morning came and the storm had not abated. It lasted all through that day, the wind ripping into the ship and sending it further and further South.

"There's never been a storm like this in my memory!" Nornos Rique said.

The others agreed.

"Further North," said Andel, "they're quite frequent. Lasting for days, so they say."

"That's true," said Sojan.

By midnight of the next night the storm finished and the sky cleared of the clinging cloud. The stars, their constellations unfamiliar to Earth eyes, shone brightly and Sojan took a quick bearing.

"We're over Shortani all right," he muttered. "Well over. In fact, I believe we're near the interior of the continent."

Beneath them the scene was one of peace rather than that of death and mystery. Great plains, watered by winding rivers, lush forests, rearing mountains, proud – like Gods looking down upon men. Here and there herds of strange animals could be detected for the moons were very bright. They were drinking and did not look up as the airship glided silently above them.

In the morning Sojan and Andel set to work on repairing the broken steering-lines whilst the others looked down at the peaceful-seeming country beneath them.

All the time they worked they drifted further and further into the interior.

"If we drift much further Sojan, we won't have enough fuel to get us out again. Remember, we only had enough for

a short journey!" Parijh called up to him where he was working on the steering gear.

"Yit take us! I hadn't thought of that," cried Sojan. "But
there's nothing we *can* do until this steering is fixed. Work as
fast as possible Andel or we'll be stranded here!"

But repairing the steering wires and readjusting the rudder,
especially sitting in the rigging with only a flimsy safety line
between you and oblivion, isn't easy and it took Sojan and
Andel several hours before the motors could be started up
again.

"There's not enough fuel to make it back to Hatnor," Sojan
said. "But if we're lucky we'll make a civilised country on the
Shortani coast!"

Now there was nothing they could do but hope and the men
relaxed, watching the wonderful scenery beneath them and
speculating on what kind of men, if any, lived there.

Red, who played a Zylorian instrument called a *rinfrit* – a
kind of eight-stringed guitar, sang them a song, based on an
old legend about these parts. The first verse went something
like this:

> "There's many a tale that has been told
> Of Phek the traveller, strong and bold!
> But the strangest one I've ever heard –
> Is when he caught a *shifla bird*."

"What's a *shifla bird*?" enquired Andel curiously.

"Oh, it's supposed to be as big as an airship and looks like
a great lizard."

His companions were amused at this story, and all but Sojan,
who was looking over towards the West, laughed.

"Don't worry too much," said Sojan calmly, "but is that
anything like your shifla bird?"

And there, rising slowly from the forest, was the largest
animal any of the adventurers had ever seen. Earth men would
call it a dragon if they saw it. Its great reptilian jaws were
agape and its huge bat-wings drove it along at incredible speed.

"It seems there was some truth in the legend," muttered

Red, licking dry lips and automatically fingering his pistol at his belt.

"There's always some truth in legends," said Sojan, "however incredible."

The thing was almost upon them now, obviously taking their cruiser for some kind of rival. It was as big as their cruiser although its body was about half the size whilst its wings made up the rest of its bulk. It was a kind of blueish grey, its great mouth a gash of crimson in its head whilst wicked eyes gleamed from their sockets making it look like some supernatural demon from the Zylorian 'Halls of the Dead'.

"Drop, Sojan, drop!" cried Nornos Rique as the men stood for a moment paralysed at this sight of something which they attributed only to the story scrolls of children.

Sojan whirled, rushed over to the controls and pushed several levers which opened valves in their gas-bag and caused the ship to lose height quickly.

The shifla swooped low overhead, barely missing them and causing them to duck automatically. Suddenly there came a crashing of branches, the ripping of fabric and the harsh snap of breaking wood. The ship had crashed into the forest. The men had been so busy trying to escape from the danger above them that they had forgotten the forest beneath them.

Sojan lifted his arm to shield his face and flung himself backwards as a branch speared through the ship as if it were a fish and nearly speared him at the same time. Eventually the noise stopped and, although the ship was swaying dangerously and threatening to fall apart any moment, sending the men to destruction, Sojan and his friends found that they had only bruises and scratches.

Sojan's barbarian instincts came to the rescue. Cat-footed as ever he clambered out of the wreckage on to the branch which had almost killed him.

"Quick," he yelled, "after me!"

His friends followed him quickly, Parijh panting with the effort. They moved cautiously along the branch and finally reached the trunk of the tree. Down they clambered, easily now for the tree was full of strong branches and it was only a drop of four or five feet to the ground.

Sojan looked up to where the airship dangled, its great gas-bag deflated, the gondola smashed and torn.

"When that falls," he said, "we'd better be some distance away for it's likely that the engine will explode."

"There go our supplies and rifles and ammunition," said Nornos Rique quietly.

"We've got our lives – for the present at least," Sojan reminded him. "We'll have to head steadily Northwards and hope that we don't strike a mountain range. If we are lucky we can follow a river across a plain. Several plains adjoin civilised or semi-civilised territories don't they, Parijh?"

"One of them runs into my own country of Uffjir, Sojan, but there's one chance in fifty of making it!"

"Then it looks as if we'll have to chance it, Parijh," Sojan replied slowly, looking over towards the East. "But at least we shall be able to ride. There – see?"

They looked in the direction in which he was pointing. About a mile away, a herd of myats grazed placidly.

"Fan out – we should catch them easily if we organise properly," Sojan called.

Slowly, so that they would not disturb the animals, Sojan and his friends closed in on the myats. Once trapped they were easily caught for, unlike most animals used as beasts of burden, myats were bred originally for the sole purpose of carrying man.

Now that they were mounted, the friends made good time in the direction in which they were headed. Some days later Sojan caught sight of a strange gleam in the distance – as if the sun was glancing off a highly polished surface.

"Head in that direction," he called to his companions. "There seems to be a building of some kind over there!"

And sure enough, it was a building. A great glistening domed construction, rising hundreds of feet, so it seemed, into the air. It was built of a similar stone to marble – but what was it? And why was it standing alone in such a savage wilderness and (this troubled the companions more than anything) were there men using it now?

"The only way to find out who or what is in there is to go nearer," said Andel.

"You're right," agreed Sojan. "Let's go!"

They forced their steeds into a quick trot.

They dismounted silently and made their way cautiously to the wide entrance of the place, which seemed to be unguarded.

There were windows high above them, seeming to be set in rooms situated at different levels in the building. Part of the roof was flat but most of it rose in a magnificent dome. Although there were no signs of corrosion at all, the men got the impression that the building was centuries old.

"There seem to be no stairs in the place," mused Sojan, looking around him at the gleaming marble hall which they had entered. To his left were two sheets of shining metal, seemingly set into the walls for no reason. To his right was an archway leading into a room just as bare as the one in which they now stood.

"Wonder what these are?" Red said, brushing his hand across one of the metal sheets.

Instantly there was a faint hum and the sheet of metal disappeared upwards, revealing a small – was it a cupboard?

Red stepped warily into the alcove, sword in hand. At once, the sheet of metal hummed downwards behind him.

"*By Yit! He's trapped!*" cried Sojan.

He brushed his own hand across the metal, but nothing happened. For several minutes he tried to open the metal door but it seemed impossible. How Red had done it, they could not tell.

Suddenly from the outside came a yell.

Rushing into the sunlight they looked up – and there was Red, looking very cheerful, grinning down on them – from a window of the tenth storey, the one nearest the roof.

"How did you get up there?" called Nornos Rique.

"The 'cupboard' took me up! It's a kind of moving box

which lifts you up to any storey you wish. Though I had to go all the way up. There were lots of buttons to press, but I dare not press any of them. After I'd got out, the doors closed again. I tried to get back in but the doors at that end wouldn't move. It looks as if I'm stuck here for life."

He didn't look as if he was particularly worried about the prospect.

Comprehending, Sojan rushed back into the great hall and again passed his hand over the metal 'door'. It hummed upwards. He didn't step in immediately but waited for his friends to join him.

"The ones who built this place must have been wonderful engineers," remarked Sojan. "And by the way, I recognised the language in which the directions for the operation of that thing were written – it's old Kifinian!"

"What?" exclaimed Parijh. "You mean that the ancestors of the Kifinians built this?"

"Obviously. Otherwise how do you explain the language?"

"From what you learned at the Temple of Rhan, Sojan," mused Nornos Rique. "The ancestors of the entire planet, so far as human beings like ourselves are concerned, came from another planet thousands of years ago – perhaps this was built before the race spread and degenerated. But what could it be?"

"I think I know," answered Sojan. "Notice how the whole area around the building is entirely treeless – a flat plain – a few shrubs, now, and other vegetation, but for the most part flat. This place was a landing field for airships of some kind. We have, as you know, similar landing fields all over the civilised parts of Zylor. This place was a control station probably."

Suddenly Red who had been standing by the window called to his friends.

"*Look, down there!*" he yelled. "*Savages, hundreds of them!*"

Below them swarmed a silent mass of strange near-human creatures. They all carried spears and short, broad-bladed swords. They were covered in short, matted hair and had long tails curling behind them.

"We seem to have violated taboo ground, judging by their actions," said Parijh who knew the people better than the rest, for his race occasionally traded with them. "They won't enter themselves, but they will wait until we come out – as come out we must, for food."

"The best thing we can do," said Andel, "is to look around this place and see if there is any other way out."

"Good idea," agreed Sojan, "if you see any more of those metal plates, try to open them."

They split up and each explored a certain section of the floor. Soon they heard Andel call from the centre of the building. Rushing to the room from which he had called they were astounded to see a large, opened panel. This one revealed a kind of bridge spanning a drop which must have gone right down to the foundations of the building. The bridge led to a huge, streamlined shell of gleaming metal fitted with triangular fins.

They stepped on to the bridge and moved single file across it until they reached a door. Scowling faintly, Sojan deciphered the ancient hieroglyphics on it.

"Here we are," he said, pressing a button. "To Open." And open it did.

"It's obviously an airship of some kind," said Andel, who was the most mechanically minded of the five. "Probably a ship similar to the ones in which our ancestors came to this planet."

"You mean an airship capable of travelling – through *space*?" said Sojan.

"Perhaps," said Andel, "but also travelling from continent to continent probably. If only we knew how to operate it!"

They finally managed to find the control room of the ship. All around them were tiers of dials and instruments. Working quickly, now that the script was becoming more familiar to him, Sojan deciphered most of the captions on the instruments. Set on the main control panel were levers marked, 'Automatic, Emergency, Poltoon', 'Automatic, Emergency, Jhar', etc. The names were those of continents.

"We can't stay here all the time," said Sojan. "If we stay we will starve to death, if we go outside we die, we might as well risk it." So saying, and without waiting for his friends' advice he pulled the lever marked Poltoon and stood back.

There came a gentle hum as the door through which they had entered closed. Another hum grew steadily louder and the entire roof of the building opened out letting in the sunlight. Then a hiss and a rumble like thunder and Sojan and his companions were thrown to the floor. Still the rumble increased until blackness overcame them and they lost consciousness.

Sojan was the first to recover. Looking through the forward porthole he saw a sight which to him was terrifying. The velvet blackness of outer space, stars set like diamonds in its ebony beauty.

There was another rumble from the depths of the ship. With animal tenacity he sought to cling to consciousness. But it was no good. He collapsed once more on the floor of the ship.

He awoke a second time to see a blue sky above him and green vegetation beneath him. His friends rose on shaky legs.

"We're not much better off, it seems," grinned Sojan — cheerful now. "We're in the Poltoonian Wilderness. The nearest civilised land is Tigurn. See, over there are the remains of a port similar to the one on the Shortani plain."

He pulled another lever. Immediately the portholes disappeared and they had the sensation of moving downwards at great velocity. A high pitched whine and they stopped. A panel slid open and a small bridge moved outwards over a drop of some five feet above the ground.

"There was probably a landing stage at this point," said Sojan with the air of an ancient professor delivering a lecture. "Anyway," he laughed, "we can drop the last few feet."

When they reached the ground they stood back.

Then the faint purr of machinery and the doors closed. Another sound, not quite so smooth — the chug-chug of an airship motor. The companions turned and saw several large airships of standard pattern circling above them. They flew the banner of Pelira, a country which had allegiance to Hatnor. Flying low, the captain of the airship inspected them, saw that they were not the strange monsters he had expected and landed his craft lightly fifty feet away from them. They ran towards it.

The look of astonishment on the captain's face was ludicrous. He immediately recognised the companions who, since their conquest of the priest-rulers of Rhan had become national heroes.

"What – what – ?" was all he could get out at first.

"How're you fixed for fuel, friend?" laughed Sojan.

"We – we've got a full tank, sir, but how . . . ?"

"Then head for Hatnor," grinned the adventurer. "We'll explain on the way."

SOJAN AND THE SONS OF THE SNAKE-GOD

(1958)

"Who seeks to set foot in Dhar-Im-Jak?"

A harsh voice rang across the harbour to the merchantman *Kintonian Trader*, which rode at anchor there.

The captain cupped his hands into a megaphone and roared back at the soldier.

"Sojan Shieldbearer, late of the court of Nornos Kad in Hatnor, mercenary swordsman! Seeking employment!"

"I've heard of him. Very well, we need good sword arms in Dhar-Im-Jak, tell him he may land!"

Traani, captain of the *Trader*, called down to Sojan who sat sprawled in his cabin.

"They say you can land, Sojan!"

"Right, I'll get my gear together."

Ten minutes later, a tall figure stepped on to the deck of the ship. His long fair hair was held back from his eyes by a fillet of metal, his dark blue eyes had a strange, humorous glint in them. Over a jerkin of green silk was flung a heavy cloak of yellow, his blue breeches were tucked into leather boots. Upon his back was slung a long and powerful air rifle, on his left arm he carried a round shield. From a belt around his waist were hung a long vilthor and a pistol holster. Sojan the Swordsman was looking for work.

Later that day, in an inn near the city centre, Sojan met the man to whom he had been directed when he had told the authorities of the harbour what kind of employment he was seeking.

"You're looking for employment in the ranks of the regular military, I hear? What qualifications do you have?" he said.

"I was commander of the Armies of Imperial Hatnor for nearly a year. In that time I succeeded in stopping a rising in Veronlam, a similar rising in Asno, I organised the Poltoonian barbarians when Nornos Kad was deposed and restored him to his throne, I and four others were instrumental in utterly destroying the would-be conquerors of Zylor – the Rhanian Theocracy. I have been involved in several minor border wars, but of late things have quietened down and I thought that I would try my luck somewhere else. I heard of the impending war between the city states of Dhar-Im-Jak and Forsh-Mai and decided that I would like to take part."

"I have heard of you, Sojan. Your remark about Rhan jogged my memory. I feel that you would be a great asset to us. We need more professional soldiers of your calibre. As you know, both Dhar-Im-Jak and Forsh-Mai have been on friendly terms for hundreds of years, neither of us had any use for regular armies. Then about a year ago this new religious cult took over the ruling of Forsh-Mai and quickly formed an army of soldiers, spies, trouble-makers and all kinds of under-cover men. It was only recently that our own spies brought us the news that, as we suspected, Forsh-Mai was preparing to march into Dhar-Im-Jak and take over our republic."

"Have you any idea when they intend to attack?"

"In two weeks' time, no less, I'm sure."

"Then we must work fast. I would be grateful to know what kind of command you intend giving me?"

"I shall have to discuss that with my superiors. I will naturally let you know as soon as possible."

Edek rose, downed the last of his drink and, with a short nod, left the inn. Just as Sojan was rising, there came a scream from the alley outside. Sword out, he rushed for the door to see a girl struggling in the grip of several burly fighting men. They were obviously bent on kidnapping her and Sojan lost no time in engaging the nearest hireling. The man was an expert swordsman, his thrusts were well timed and it was all Sojan could do, at first, to parry them. The man's companions were still holding the girl who seemed to be making no attempt to get free. The clash of steel was music to him and a grim fighting smile appeared on his lips. Suddenly he felt a hard blow on the back of his head and the lights went out.

He regained consciousness in a small room, barred on both door and windows. Standing over him were two men; one held a water jug in his hand with which he was dousing Sojan.

"So our hard-headed mercenary is at last awake, I see!" The tone was gloating. The man's face did not belie the impression his voice gave. His thick black locks and beard were curled and oiled.

Upon his fingers were heavy rings, his nails were tinted with gold. Sojan looked at him in disgust. The bejewelled fop signalled to his companion to throw some more water at Sojan. Instantly Sojan rose and knocked the jug flying across the small cell.

"If your manners were as fine as the silks you wear, my friend, I should take you for *some* sort of man!"

The fop's face twisted for a moment and he half raised his hand. Then he smiled and dropped the hand to his side.

"We'll allow the wolf some time in which to cool the heat of his temper as water seems to be no use," he murmured. "Come, Yuckof, let us leave this place – it smells!"

Sojan signalled to the guard who was locking the door.

"What place is this, friend?"

"You're in the Castle of Yerjhi, swordsman, we caught you nicely didn't we? That ruse in getting a girl to pretend that she was being captured was Lord Yerjhi's idea. He's a clever one. You'd be better off to be a little more civil to him, he is thinking of employing you."

Several hours later, Yerjhi returned with the same escort.

"Now, Sojan," he smiled, "I can understand your annoyance at being locked up in this place – but it was the only way in which we could – um – convince you of our sincerity when we offer you fifty thousand *derkas* to take command of our armies and lead them to glorious victory for the State of

Forsh-Mai. We, the Sons of the Snake, will conquer all. Everything will be yours. What say you man, is that not a fair proposition?"

"Aye, it's fair," Sojan's eyes narrowed. He decided to bluff for a while. "*Fifty* thousand you say?"

"That and any spoils you can take for yourself when we loot Dhar-Im-Jak!"

"But what's this 'Sons of the Snake' you mention? Do I have to join some secret society to wield a sword for fifty thousand derkas?"

"That is a necessary part of our offer, Sojan. We are, after all, doing this for the glory of Rij, the Snake, Lord of the World and the After World, Master of Darkness, Ruler of the . . ."

"Yes, yes, we'll forget that for a moment. What does it involve?"

"First a meeting of all the major disciples, myself, the General-in-Command (who will take orders from you while the conquest is in progress), my major-domo, the two priests who invent – hem – who spread the Truth of the Snake."

"But why this mumbo-jumbo – if you want to conquer your enemy, why not just do it? I can't understand what you're trying to do."

"Then briefly I will explain. The two cities have been at peace for hundreds of years. Men and women from the states have intermingled with each other, intermarried. Apart from the names and boundaries, we are practically the same people. We need an excuse, man, don't you see? We can't send a man to march against his brother or even son unless he thinks that there is something worth fighting for. This, my dear Sojan, is a – hem – Holy War. Quite legitimate. We are – how shall I put it? – spreading the Word of the Snake God with the Sword of Justice! Part of our indoctrination campaign, actually. that last bit.'

"Right! I'll join," Sojan had hit on a daring plan. "When do I become an initiate?"

An hour later, Sojan stood in a darkened room. In front of

him was a long table and at it sat men clad in robes decorated with serpents.

"Let the ceremony begin," he intoned.

Now was the time to act. They had given Sojan back his sword along with his other equipment and he now drew it. With the blade humming he downed the two nearest men. Three left, three wary men and led by one who had been described as the finest swordsman in Shortani.

Luckily only two of the men were swordsmen – the other was almost helpless. In the fore Yerjhi, cowl flung back and his face a mask of hate.

"Trick me would you," he hissed. "We'll show you what we do to dogs who try to turn on Yerjhi!"

Sojan felt a lancing pain go through him and he felt the warm blood as it trickled down his left arm. With renewed energy he launched himself at Yerjhi who was taken off guard for a moment. Clean steel pierced a tainted heart and the man toppled backwards with a short death-scream.

With the fake 'Sons of the Snake God' exposed for what they were, what amounted to civil war was averted and the two cities resumed their friendly relations. Once again Sojan had done a major service for a cause in which he believed.

SOJAN AND THE DEVIL HUNTERS OF NORJ

(1958)

The last rays of Zylor's second sun were just waning when Sojan reined his myat and stared down into the green valley below.

He glanced at the crude map before him.

"This must be the Valley of Norj. It seems to be unexplored according to the map. Strange that no one has ventured into it."

Strange it was; for, even in the dusk, Sojan could see that the valley was lush and green. A river wound through it and brightly plumed birds sang from the branches of tall trees. A seeming paradise.

"It will make an excellent place to camp," thought the mercenary as he guided his mount downwards.

Later that night, he made his camp in a small natural clearing in the forest. His myat was tethered nearby and his campfire glowed cheerily. The night was warm and full of forest smells.

After eating his meal, Sojan climbed between his blankets and was soon asleep.

It was just after midnight when the strange noises awakened the warrior.

There they were again – a peculiar hissing screech and the pounding of hooves; the cries of – men, and the vicious cracks of whips.

Sojan raised himself on one elbow, hand reaching for his sword. The myat stirred uneasily and swished its great tail from side to side.

The noises drew nearer and then subsided as they fell away towards the West of the valley.

Sojan did not sleep any more that night but kept a watchful eye open. The rest of the night was uneventful and in the morning, Sojan cooked himself a big meal which was meant to last him the day, for he intended to investigate the noises he had heard, the night before.

Riding slowly, with eyes always scanning the ground, Sojan soon found the tracks that the inhabitants of the valley had made. There were two distinct sets of tracks. One similar to those of a myat although with subtle differences, seemingly lighter. The others were entirely unfamiliar. Three-toed tracks like, and yet unlike, those of a bird – and considerably larger. The beast that had made them was obviously a quadruped of some kind, but other than that Sojan could not tell what kind of animal had made them – there were few four-legged birds he could think of – and none of the ones he had heard about were as large as this.

There had been at least ten riders, and it seemed that they had been chasing one or perhaps two of these bird-beasts. Probably some kind of hunt, thought Sojan, yet what kind of men were they who hunted at the dead of night?

Sojan rode on, following the tracks in the hope that he would find some clue to the mystery. He came across a steep inclination, the tracks ended here in a flurry of mud and – blood. Then the tracks of the beasts the men had been riding continued, and they had ridden for a short while parallel with the bluff and then forced their animals to ride up it.

Sojan did the same, the beast slipped occasionally and nearly slid back but eventually it reached the top. From there Sojan saw a strange scene.

A battle of some kind was going on between two groups of men. Near a squat black-stoned tower, five men, one mounted, were endeavouring to check a horde of armoured warriors who rushed from the tower. Beasts similar to Sojan's myat but hornless and almost tailless stood waiting.

The mounted man held the tethering reins of the other four

animals while he cut at two of the armoured men with a battleaxe held in his right hand.

Although the mounted man was clad in armour, the other four were dressed only in jerkins of coloured cloth and divided kilts of leather. They were unshod and carried no sheaths for the weapons, mainly swords, with which they defended themselves. It seemed to Sojan that they were attempting to escape from the armoured warriors, one of whom, dressed more richly, and darker than the others, stood in the rear and urged them on in a language which was unfamiliar, yet strangely familiar, to Sojan's ears.

But there was no time to ponder over this now; the men needed help and Sojan, in a more curious than chivalrous mood, intended to aid them and perhaps find some answer to the mystery.

His long spear was out, his shield up and he forced the myat into a wild gallop down the hill, screaming to his gods in a barbarian war-shout.

His savage thrust caught the first of the armoured warriors in the throat and stayed there, the spear jerking like a tufted reed in a storm. His sword screamed from its scabbard as he pushed deeper into the melée of cursing men.

Taking this chance of escape while the enemy were still confused, the other men quickly mounted their beasts. Sojan was still in the thick of it, sword lashing everywhere and dealing death with every stroke. One of the riders looked back, saw the mercenary still engaged and spurred his own beast back to where Sojan fought.

Grinning his thanks to Sojan he covered the mercenary's retreat with his own slim blade then followed.

Howling, the warriors attempted to pursue on foot, were brought back by their Leader's frantic cries and scrambled round the back of the building.

The armoured rider called to Sojan in the familiar, yet unintelligible tongue, and pointed towards the East. Sojan understood and turned his myat in that direction. Behind them their pursuers were whipping their steeds in an effort to overtake them.

Deep into the forest they rode, leaving their enemies far behind. For perhaps three hours they detoured until they reached the end of the valley where a sheer cliff rose. Brushing aside some shrubbery, the armoured man disclosed an opening in the base of the cliff.

Ducking their heads, the six rode through, the last man replacing the camouflage.

The passage ended in several connecting caves and it was in one of these that they stabled their mounts and continued on foot to the cave at the far end. Here they slumped into chairs, grinning with relief at their escape.

The leader, the man in armour, began to speak to Sojan who stood bewilderedly trying to understand the language in which they questioned him. Vaguely he began to realise what it was – it was his own tongue, yet so altered as to be scarcely recognisable. In an hour he could understand most of their speech and in two he was telling them how he had come to the Valley of Norj.

"But I am curious to find out who you are – and why men hunt giant four-legged birds at midnight," he said. "Who were the men from whom you escaped?"

"It is a long story to explain in a few words," said Jarg, the leader, "but I will first attempt to tell you a little of the political situation here, in Norj.

"There are two distinct races living here – men like ourselves – and – another race whom I scarcely like to define as 'men'. Ages ago our people reached this valley after a long sea voyage and trek across Shortani. We came to this valley and settled in it and it was not for some time that we learned that another people lived at the far end of the valley. A race of grim, black-haired and black-eyed men, who hunted at night with steel-tipped flails and who remained in their castles during the day. They did not trouble us at first and eventually we became used to the hunts, even though they sometimes passed through our fields and destroyed our crops. We were secure, we thought, in the valley and there was no man curious enough to venture too near the black-stoned castles of the Cergii.

"But soon men and women – even children – of our people began to disappear and the hunts became more frequent for the Cergii had found a new sport – a different quarry to the Devil-birds which they breed and release at night to hunt with their whips. It was then that the mangled bodies of our tribesmen began to be found – lashed to death.

"They were capturing our people – and hunting them! So it was that we declared war upon these beasts, these whom we had never harmed nor attempted to harm.

"Over the years traitors to our race went over to the enemy and became their warriors – you saw some of them today – our once great race dwindled – and became fugitives, living in caves and – if captured – the quarry of the Hunters of Norj. Still we carry on warfare with them – but it is hit and run fighting at best. The four you see here were captured recently and it was more by luck than anything that I managed to bribe a guard to release them. I came last night with weapons and myats – you see that the breed has changed as has our speech. Unfortunately the timing was imperfect and the first sun arose before we could make good our escape. We were seen and would all be dead or captured had it not been for you."

"There must be some way to defeat them!" cried Sojan. "And if there is a way – I swear that I will find it!"

Sojan and the fighting men of Norj, some sixty in all, stood in the main cave, waiting for nightfall.

Plans of Sojan's attempt to overcome the Cergii, who hunted men with steel-tipped flails, had been discussed and Sojan and Jarg, the leader, had reached a decision.

The Cergii were few, it seemed, about ten in number. They were immortal, or at least their life-spans were incredibly long and the race had gradually dwindled to ten evil sorcerer-warriors whose only pleasure was the midnight hunts.

At dusk, Sojan rose, went over the final plan with his friends, and left, heading Eastwards towards the castles of the Cergii — some twenty in all, mostly in an advanced state of decay — only one of which housed the Cergii and their Norjian slaves and hirelings.

The tiny Zylorian moons gave scant light and Sojan found it difficult picking his way through the rubble of the ruined outbuildings.

There came a faint scuffling behind him; a sound which only a barbarian's senses could have heard.

Sojan ignored it and carried on.

Even when the scuffling came nearer he ignored it. The sudden blow on the back of his head was impossible to ignore, however, and a blind sense of survival set him wheeling round, hand groping for his sword hilt before blackness, deeper than night swam in front of his eyes and he lost consciousness.

He awoke in a damp-smelling cell, lit only by torchlight which filtered through a tiny grill in the wall. The cell was obviously on a corner for the large barred door was not in the same wall as the grill.

Peering throught this door was an unkempt warrior clad in dirty armour and holding a spear.

He glared short-sightedly at the mercenary with half-mad eyes. His mouth gaped open showing bad teeth and he chuckled loudly.

"You're the next game for the Hunters of Cergii," he cackled. "Oh! What a feast the beasts will have tonight."

Sojan ignored these words, turned over and attempted to ease the pain in his aching head.

After many hours in which he attempted to get some rest, Sojan was jabbed roughly awake by the guard's spear butt.

"What is it now?" he enquired as he raised himself to his feet and dusted off the straw in which he'd been sleeping.

"Heh, heh!" cackled the man. "It's almost midnight — time for one of our little hunts!"

Sojan became tense. He had a plan based on the knowledge that if he was captured he would most certainly be forced to partake in one of the hunts of the Cergii – as the quarry.

"Very well," he said, trying to sound as frightened as possible.

The courtyard was dark and gloomy, one moon showing through a gap in the ruins. The strange smell of an unknown animal came to Sojan's nostrils and he gathered that these were the 'hounds' of the Cergii that Jarg had told him about.

He heard the stamping of the myats' hooves and the jingle of harness and, as his eyes became accustomed to the darkness, made out the vague outlines of tall mounted men.

"Is the quarry ready?" called out a voice as dead and cold as the ruins around them.

"Yes, Master, he is here!"

"Then tell him that he will be given quarter of an hour's start – then we will be upon his scent!" the voice went on.

The guards stood aside and Sojan was off – along a route already planned nights ago. His plan was a daring one and one which called for a great deal of courage. He was acting as a human snare for the Hunters.

Down a narrow forest trail he ran, the trees and grasses rustling in the cold night breeze, the sound of small animals calling to each other and the occasional scream as a larger animal made its kill.

The air in his lungs seemed to force itself out as he ran faster and faster. The time was getting short and he had several more minutes yet until he could reach the agreed spot.

Sounds – not the sounds of the forest, but more ominous – began to reach his ears. The sounds of cracking whips and thundering hooves as the Hunters and their silent hounds rode in pursuit.

Faster and faster he ran keeping his eyes open for the landmark which would afford him comparative safety.

At last it came into sight, just as the cracking of whips and pounding hooves seemed to be on top of him. Past the tall rock he ran, into a tiny gorge flanked on each side by towering rock walls.

Up the side of the cliff he scrambled as the Hunters entered the gorge. Then :

"Now !" roared Sojan, and as he did so sixty death-tipped arrows flew down and buried themselves in the bodies of many of the Cergii.

Their curses and frantic screams were music to Sojan and his friends as they fitted new arrows and let fly at the sounds.

Sojan leapt down the rocks again, a long sword in his right hand.

A shadowy rider loomed out of the darkness and an evil face, white teeth flashing in a grin of triumph, aimed a blow at Sojan with his own blade.

Sojan cut upwards, catching the rider in the leg. He screamed and tumbled off his steed, putting it between himself and Sojan.

He came upright, limping rapidly in the mercenary's direction. Sojan ducked another savage cut and parried it. Down lunged his opponent's sword attempting to wound Sojan's sword-arm. He again parried the stroke and counter-thrust towards the man's chest.

Following up this move with a thrust to the heart, the mercenary ended the evil hunter's life.

Most of the Cergii were now either dead or mortally wounded and it did not take Sojan and his friends long to finish off the job they had started.

"Now for their hirelings !" yelled Sojan, goading his myat in the direction from which he had come; his sword dripping red in the moonlight, his hair tousled and a wildness in his eyes.

The sixty riders thundered down the narrow forest trail towards the castles of the dead Cergii, Sojan at their head, voicing a battle-cry which had been shouted at a dozen great victories for the men whom Sojan had led.

Straight into the courtyard they swarmed, catching the soldiers entirely unawares.

Dismounting, they crashed open the doors of the castle and poured in.

"Guard the doors!" yelled Sojan. "And all other exits – we'll exterminate every traitor in the place!"

His first call was in the dungeons – for there he knew he would find the man who had been his jailer during the previous day.

The half-crazed warrior cringed when he saw Sojan enter sword in hand. But one look at the tall mercenary told him that he could expect no mercy.

Drooling with fear he yanked his own sword from its scabbard and swung a blow at Sojan which would have cut him in two had it not been deflected by Sojan's blade.

Coolly Sojan fought while his opponent became more and more desperate.

Slowly the warrior was forced back as Sojan's relentless sword drove him nearer and nearer the wall.

His madness gave him immense stamina and gradually he began to fight with more skill.

"Heh, heh!" he cackled, "you will soon die man! Think not that you escaped death when you escaped the Cergii!"

Sojan smiled a grim smile and said nothing.

Suddenly the maddened warrior wrenched a spear from the wall and hurled it at Sojan. It plunked heavily into his left arm causing him to gasp with pain.

Then his eyes hardened and the warrior read his fate in them.

"You'll die for that," said Sojan calmly.

Almost immediately the warrior went down before a blurring network of steel and died with an inch of steel in his throat.

Sojan returned to the main hall of the castle where his friends were finishing off the rest of the Cergii's warriors.

"Well," he laughed cheerfully, "I must be off!"

Jag turned. He saw the wound inflicted by the madman's spear.

"You can't ride in that state, Sojan!" he cried.

"Oh it will heal," Sojan smiled. "It is only a superficial cut! But you have work to do, restoring your farms now that the Cergii are vanquished. I should like to stay – but this is an interesting continent with lots to see. If I hurry I might be able to see it all before I die!"

With that he strode from the room, mounted his myat and cantered off, up the steep track which led out of the valley of Norj.

"There goes a brave man!" murmured Jag as he watched him disappear over the hill-top.

KLAN THE SPOILER

(1958)

Screaming a battle-cry a blond giant, broadsword cutting an arc of steel before him, crashed through the window.

Nizriff of Gulipht shrank back, cowering on his padded couch, terror in his eyes.

"Where is she, you scum?" Klan roared. "By the Gods, if you've harmed her – "

"No, Klan, no – she's safe enough, this I swear. She – she – lies in the lower dungeon of the castle, but she is well cared for, I promise you!"

"Which castle, man? Am I to hunt in every castle on the planet?"

"Urjohl of Civ – his castle, Klan. The one on the island of Civ. Urjohl's own castle. Please, Klan, I know no more . . ."

Klan ran up the long ladder on to the deck and bellowed orders through a megaphone.

"Set a course for Civ!" he yelled. "We must get to Civ within a day!"

"But that's impossible, sir," cried the mate.

"Then make it possible, man. There's more at stake than spoils in this voyage."

A day later found them nearing Civ and here Klan told the ship to anchor. Then, taking only a sword and knife, he slipped into a small skiff and rowed the remaining miles to disembark on an uninhabited part of the island.

An hour's walk found him within sight of the Castle of Civ, its harsh towers rising above the damp ground mist. Almost impregnable, it seemed a solid block of rock squatting on the low hills like some ancient armoured monster.

How to enter was the thing which had been troubling Klan ever since he heard that Sherahl had been imprisoned here. These castles, though not very pleasant to look at, were so well-built and guarded that few enemies, however ingenious, could gain entrance.

Suddenly a low growl behind him, caused Klan to wheel.

A swamp cat, jaws wide, showing razor-sharp teeth, stood ready to spring.

Instantly Klan reacted. Instead of leaping away, he jumped towards the great beast, his sword held in front of him like a spear. Straight into the beast's mouth it slid, tearing into it like a ship into water.

The hideous scream of the monster cat seemed to combine the ear-splitting shriek of a train whistle with the deafening roar of its engines.

But it died, and Klan was safe for the moment. Then another thought – had the death-scream been heard by the Castle? Obviously it had, for shouts reached his ears.

"Is anyone down there?" called a voice. "What's the trouble?"

Klan hugged the walls of the castle and made no answer. Soon the castle gate opened a little and a wary column of armoured men crept from it, eyes staring into the gloom, seeing little but the swirling, ever-present, mist.

The last man in the column was the unlucky one. Strong arms reached out of the mist and hauled him down into the mud choking the breath from him until he lay unconscious on the swampy ground. Quickly, Klan bound and gagged him, stripped his uniform from him and donned it himself. Then he returned to the gate and banged on it until a panel was pulled back; he was inspected and finally let in.

"What happened?" enquired the guard. "Is there an enemy out there?"

"If there was, there isn't now," Klan answered truthfully.

Even in the castle courtyard, the grey mist swirled so that the guard could not make out his features clearly.

Striding to the steps leading up to the main part of the building, Klan ran up them and entered one of the dark corridors so typical of castles of this type.

Risking everything he halted a female servant who was passing.

"Hey, woman," he muttered. "Where's Urjohl now?"

"Where he usually is at this hour," she replied brusquely, "in the top room of the main tower!"

Up the stairs to the top room. No time for subterfuge now, he must . . .

"Stay where you are, my friend! If you move, you'll be pitched into a bottomless well!"

Klan looked up. There in the ceiling was a small trapdoor – and looking through it was the evil face of Urjohl of Civ. As Klan looked up, Urjohl recognised him.

"Ah, my good friend Klan of Karahl calling upon me. I am very pleased to see you. Your sister is staying with us at present. No doubt you wish to join her? Well that can be arranged." The gloating face disappeared from the trap as it closed but the voice added: "And I don't advise you to move at all. If you attempt to shift your weight the paving stone upon which you stand will give way and you will be hurled down a shaft which, as far as we know, leads to – infinity."

Klan dare not risk moving. Urjohl might be bluffing but there was no way of testing apart from the obvious one.

Soon he heard the tramp of feet on the stairway and a number of armoured guards surrounded him.

The voice was heard again.

"Right, you may all enter now."

Klan was pushed into a richly furnished room, one of the few splashes of colour in the dark castle. A huge fire reared in the grate and in one corner, her hands tied behind her but otherwise looking unharmed was:

"Sherahl!" cried Klan. "What has the spawn of the swamps done to you?"

"Nothing, Klan, apart from imprisoning me in a vile cell. He expects me to marry him — faugh! I'd rather marry a swamp cat, at least they have courage!"

"Good for you, Sherahl," laughed Klan.

"Laugh now, Karahl," hissed Urjohl. 'You'll be crying for mercy, both of you, when I'm done!"

"You seem to forget that I have a fleet of ships lying off shore, Urjohl. They have only to wait another hour before they sail for Civ and destroy your castle utterly."

"You bluff, Klan, you have but one ship lying off Civ — and even now my own fleet goes to sink it. Your tortures will not be made bearable by hope, my friend!"

"Then it's only myself I can rely upon!" yelled the spoiler and leapt for the throat of the Civite, throwing him completely off balance. The guards rushed forward to save their master but by this time Klan's sword was out and carving an arc of blue steel around him. A guard which few could break. Down went one of the three men, his throat cut by a savage slash. Urjohl remained where he lay, stark terror replacing the gloating look of triumph he had had a few moments ago. Sherahl was helpless, her hands tied. Back towards her, Klan edged, his sword licking out to deal wounds to his opponents. Drawing the knife from his sash he called to Sherahl to turn her hands towards him. Not daring to relax his guard he slashed once — and the bonds fell away. Sherahl snatched the knife and rushed towards Urjohl.

"That for the discomfort you caused me!" she cried as the dagger sank deep into the villain's heart.

Klan quickly defeated his adversaries and sheathed his bloodstained sword.

"We must hurry now to warn the ship of their danger!" he said to Sherahl. "Quickly, out of this room and down the stairs."

Down the stairs they ran and out into the courtyard.

"Hey there, stop!"

It was the guard.

Klan cut him down with one sword stroke and carried on

to the gate, Sherahl following. Picking her up, he fled into the squelching swamp lands towards his skiff.

At last he made it. Bundling his sister into the tiny boat, he unshipped the oars and put to sea with powerful strokes.

He was only minutes ahead of the Civite fleet.

As he and his sister were helped aboard he gave orders for the ship to turn about.

"There's a fleet of Civite ships on our tail," he yelled. "They'll be here at any moment!"

Quickly the ship turned and sped for open waters, and a few moments later the enemy rounded the headland and, sighting her, went all out to catch up with the fleeing vessel.

But the *Pride of Karahl* was no ordinary ship and Klan soon put a comfortable distance between their ship and those of the enemy.

"Where do we sail now, Klan?" asked Risho, the mate, a tall black-bearded man and a kinsman of Klan's.

"Head for the edge of the world," exclaimed Klan. "We'll see what new spoils can be found where no civilised man has ever been!"

(Written c. 1955)

DEK OF NOOTHAR

(1957)

Ancient Mars bred many legends, the greatest of which deals
with the mystic Sword of Life. This Sword had the power to
render a person immune to illness and old age as well as to
improve the skill in fighting on the part of the holder.

Dek of Noothar was the son of a man who had taken it
upon himself to secure this fabled Sword and bring it back to
civilisation where it could do countless deeds of mercy. His
father had died after returning to his home in the form of a
gibbering maniac, his mind having been killed by the terrible
powers of hypnotic suggestion held by the Keepers of the Sword
– The Strange Ones.

Now Dek had sworn to own the Sword or die as had his
father. He would take none with him upon the sea journey
which would bring him to the Island of the Strange Ones.

Strapping on his own sword, a weapon in the use of which
he was highly skilled, Dek embarked upon the adventure
which was to bring him close to death so many times.

The one-man skiff in which he had chosen to make the
journey was propelled by a single sail which could be raised
or lowered at will. In the skiff were packed several small
carcasses of roasted meat, bread and gourds of water. The latter
he treasured above all else.

And so Dek of Noothar sped out into the open sea on the
course that his father had taken twenty years before.

On the third day he met with a great sea-monster, fully
twenty feet in length. It resembled a massive snake but had

the gaping head of a crocodile which held a set of dangerously sharp teeth.

Standing precariously in the small boat he slashed at the creature's head with his light sword, but more often than not the incredibly agile thing darted away, then came back to snap at the man's body. Several times had Dek come near to losing his balance and being precipitated into the surrounding sea, where he would be at the mercy of the marine creature. At last by a clever move, Dek caused the thing's body to lay across the boat. With all his mighty strength the man brought his weapon down upon the slimy neck. The head rolled to the bottom of the skiff while the body, still writhing, slid back into the sea.

Laughing in relief, Dek tossed the remains overboard. Suddenly his laughter ceased. He looked up at the sky. Great black clouds were beginning to form, this was what he had feared most of all – a storm was imminent.

The sea grew calm until not a sound was to be heard. Then came a peal of thunder from above and the wind began to freshen, small droplets of rain began to fall; these grew in size as did the wind until the craft was seemingly in the middle of a boiling cauldron. The man clung to the slender mast and cursed the elements.

The storm seemed to grow in fury during the next few hours, yet the skiff, being exceptionally light, was never caught under a wave and did not take much water.

Dek, hugging the bottom of the boat, did not see the raging waves renting their fury against the rocky shores of an island ahead. The first hint of this danger that he received was when a black, jagged rock ploughed its way through the hull of the boat.

Dek, seeing the situation at a glance, and knowing what damage the rocks could still do, dived overboard into the white-flecked surf. He was rushed along toward the dark shores with the speed of a torpedo. Soon, feeling rough sand brushing his chest, he jumped to his feet and ran for the safety of the land.

SOJAN

He sheltered in one of the many caves which dotted the coastline, and slept there until morning. This, he knew, could not be his destination for he had been travelling for only three days and it took at least two weeks to reach the Strange Ones' shores.

It was late morning when he awoke, and he felt extremely hungry and thirsty. The only access to the island's interior seemed to be over the cliffs which surrounded the side of the island upon which fate had thrown him. His own country being mountainous, he was quite as much at home scaling precipitous heights as he was walking a level surface. Therefore it was with ease that he climbed over the edge of the cliff and stood about two hundred feet above the surging sea.

He stood upon the plateau, the middle of which appeared to have been scooped out. He chose to walk around the edge of this plateau, and after a few miles he found that for which he sought. A small stream trickled over the edge of the cliffs and cascaded down into the surf beneath. With this also was a large group of trees which supplied him with fruit.

While feasting from the abundant fruits he noticed to his surprise several dug-out canoes; to each was attached a long fibre rope which, surmised Dek, was used for lowering the craft into the sea below.

During his inspection of these canoes his attention was caught by the rustle of leaves at his rear. Spinning around he faced the origin of the noise. There confronted him a party of about twenty men. Their bodies were covered in a thin coat of hair and were covered, as was Dek, with a loin-cloth of fur. Each held a wicked-looking hatchet.

Dek flung himself to the ground as one of these came flying towards him. It hissed past his ear.

Convinced of their attitude toward him, Dek drew his knife. One of the creatures, motioning the rest to remain where they were, advanced upon the stranger with upraised axe.

With a savage yell the beast charged, head down; like a snake the other side-stepped and avoided the collision. The creature wheeled about in a frenzy, again it charged but this time it was not tricked. The two thudded to the hard ground.

Dek found his opponent unbelievably strong, and he knew that he could never win by brute strength alone, therefore he resorted to cunning and skill. Slowly his feet crept under the other's stomach. The creature was now trying to use its teeth on Dek and the Nootharian's mighty biceps were quivering under the straining body.

Suddenly the beast became aware of the man's intentions but it was too late. Dek's leg muscles contracted and the creature was sent flying through the air to land with a thud upon the very edge of the cliff. Not losing such a chance, Dek lunged at the rising body. With a shrill scream it was toppled from the cliff and sent spinning into the raging waters beneath.

The victor stood and looked at the falling body for a few seconds, then he spun about to face a new menace. The remaining men were moving toward him. Knowing that he could never win against such odds he looked about for some way of escape; his eyes wandered to the canoes. In his mind was forming a wild plan.

Quickly he untied the lowering rope, and pushed one of the dug-outs over the cliff-edge. The creatures cried out and started into an awkward run. They were nearly upon him now. Picking up his late opponent's axe he flung it into the on-coming faces, then dived from the cliff.

Below he saw the sea swirling around black rocks, and being tossed about like a twig, was the canoe.

Down he plunged into the white foam, down still until his lungs cried out for air; slowly he rose to the surface – so slowly. It was with surprise that Dek felt life-giving air again surround his head.

A few yards from him bobbed the canoe – he struck out for this and was soon climbing into its hollow bole. In this he found secured a crude paddle with which he sent the craft racing for the open sea.

As he looked back towards those inhospitable shores which

he had just, so hastily quitted, he wondered what other adventures would cross his path before he reached the Island of the Strange Ones.

THE SIEGE OF NOOTHAR

"It's hopeless, Dek," sighed Saroc, uncle to Dek, ruler of Noothar. "The Tarsorian legions surround the city and it is but time before our food supplies are exhausted. What is there to do but surrender to that tyrant Foona and trust to his mercy?"

"No! by the Gods, I'll never surrender, 'twould be better to die of hunger than to agree to his terms. The people of Noothar, slaves! No. Never."

"What other alternative is there? You could never surrender Tarli, your sister, to that wretch as he asks, even if it would mean the deliverance of Noothar."

"No, the people wouldn't let her go any more than I would."

Suddenly, there broke into the candle-lit chamber, a warrior, whose trappings denoted a high position in the Princess Tarli's retinue.

"What is it, Garl? Why, you look even more worried than I feel," smiled Dek dryly.

"Sir, I have good reason for worrying. The princess has disappeared."

The two men were on their feet, eyes wide.

'Disappeared," gasped Saroc, "where man?"

"Sir, a horse bearing a hooded rider was sighted leaving the city, a while ago."

"Gods!" cursed Dek. "Yes, she said she would sacrifice anything for Noothar, and this is what she meant. The little fool! Does she think that Foona will keep his word and retreat?"

He thought for a minute, then snatching down his harness, which held the fabulous Sword of Life that he had rescued from the Place of The Strange Ones a year or so back, he barked a command to the warrior.

"Have my horse and ten of my best men ready at the main gate in two minutes."

The man turned and sprinted from the room to do his ruler's bidding.

"What is your plan, my son?" queried Saroc.

"My plan," came the reply, "I have none, other than to rescue Tarli from that heathen cur."

Buckling on his weapons, Dek left the room and ran down the well-worn steps to the torch-lit courtyard where his orders had been caried out. Ten bronze-skinned men sat astride ten black horses.

Dek outlined his scant plan to the men who nodded approvingly. Then, with a clatter of hooves on the flagging, the little party cantered through the gate.

Dek knew the surrounding terrain by heart and he led his men through a narrow gully which completely hid them from the alien forces. He could have escaped the city at any time during the last week but he could never have deserted his people.

The little group emerged from the gully behind the Tarsorian lines and looked over the ranks which encircled the beleaguered city.

A yellow moon lit the scene and shone on silver helmets and sharp steel.

Below the ridge on which the riders sat there was erected a large tent which stood behind the main line – the headquarters of the force. In the tent there probably rested Foona of Tarsor. Dek gripped the hilt of his sword tighter and cursed beneath his breath.

He called his men about him and spoke in low tones.

"From here I go alone. You will stay here. If I need you I will sound my horn."

Saluting his men, he swung his mount towards the encampment and the two thousand men that constituted the Tarsorian legions.

Having tethered his horse twenty yards away he moved cautiously forward until he was at the back of the tent. He heard the sounds of voices within but could not make out the words. Drawing his dagger from its sheath, he made a slit in the canvas large enough for him to look through and hear the conversation.

The tent had two occupants. One of these was Foona. Although Dek had never seen the man before, he knew that it could be no other. Often he had been told about the cold, slanting eyes and cruel mouth surmounting a pointed beard.

The other person was well known to Dek. It was Tarli, his sister. Tarli was speaking.

"Are you saying that you will not call off the siege as you said if I was delivered to you?"

"Exactly, my dear. However much I may have wanted to meet you, I wanted the riches which are within those walls even more."

Tarli loosed a stream of abuse at the man. She raised her hand to strike but he was too quick and a powerful hand gripped her wrist.

Dek's eyes widened in rage at this. He plunged his knife into the fabric and slashed a hole large enough to admit his body. At the noise the Tarsorian spun about to find himself facing a naked blade in the hand of a man whom he had imagined to be still within the marble walls of Noothar.

With a cry of terror, he fled from the tent, shouting for his warriors.

"Come," said Dek, grasping his sister by the arm, "this is no place for you."

Once outside the tent, he loosed a horn from his trappings and sent three blasts towards the ridge. A few seconds later, the warriors of Noothar galloped up. Dek lifted Tarli on to the back of one of his captain's horses as if she weighed nothing.

"Take the Princess back to Noothar," he said. "I go to settle a score."

With that he sprang on to his own mount and galloped back towards the encampment.

Looking through the foliage of a tree, he saw his quarry issuing hasty orders to a group of about twenty warriors. A minute later they spurred their horses on to the trail that the Nootharians had taken.

Foona was alone. Dek smiled grimly as he slid from his mount. Brushing the leaves aside he stepped into the clearing.

Foona stepped back a pace in surprise.

"Your men have gone, sifla," spat Dek, "and you are about to die."

"I think not, Nootharian, none have bested Foona with a sword."

Dek advanced slowly, his weapon held at the ready. Foona drew his blade and stood his ground. For half a minute, the two master swordsmen circled each other cautiously, each looking for an opening. Foona straightened suddenly and swung a vicious cut at his opponent's head. Dek parried skilfully and returned the cut.

There ensued a battle of cautious, well thought-out moves, neither dared to take risks, for both respected the other's skill.

As the minutes rolled by, the fighting became slower on the part of Foona. Dek being the stronger, hardly felt the exhaustion that was overcoming the other.

Both, by this time, were covered in blood from the multitude of minor cuts that had been inflicted.

It was after thirty minutes that Foona made the biggest and last mistake of his life. He decided that he could not hope to prevail using plain swordsmanship, so he resorted to one of those tricks for which he was famous. After a wicked thrust at his opponent's body, he drew a knife from his harness with his left hand. Carefully he slipped it backwards until it rested in his palm. Then he flicked it forward straight for Dek's chest. But the Nootharian had seen the other's move and as it flew towards him, he swung his blade and struck it to the ground.

With a bellow of rage and disappointment, Foona flung himself into one final assault. He sprang forward with upraised blade. As he brought it down with a force that would have split his opponent from head to chest had it hit him, Dek stepped to one side, then he lunged.

Foona stopped in midstride. He straightened up, gave one choked cry and plummeted forward, three inches of cold steel protruding from his back.

Dek leant against a tree, gasping for several minutes, then he heard the sounds of the returning Tarsorian warriors. Weak from exhaustion and loss of blood, he stumbled forward to the corpse and jerked his blade from it. Replacing this in its scabbard, he staggered to where his horse stood, peacefully cropping the greenery in the soil. Painfully he pulled himself on to its back.

At a command from its master, the animal cantered off, over the ridge, back to Noothar.

The following day the force, which had previously surrounded the city, withdrew back to Tarsor, for the heart was gone out of the men. Only their late ruler's promises and threats had made them embark upon the siege which none of them had wished for.

Again the people of Noothar were free, thanks to the courage and sword arm of Dek of Noothar . . .

(*with John Wisdom*)

RENS KARTO OF BERSNOL

(1958)

"What do you make of this, Skortan?" asked the tall, dark-haired man of his centaur-like companion.

"I dare not think," answered the chieftain of Darksik in almost a whisper, "unless we're dead and we're in Frejh, the Dark Land!"

Rens Karto, Leader of the Hosts of Besna had been discussing a plan of campaign with his great friend and ally when suddenly, with no warning of any kind, they had found themselves on an alien planet under a strange, unfamiliar sun.

The Host-Leader turned to survey the landscape. "Xon's Sons! Look at that, Skortan!"

It was a great insect, coloured in hues which were entirely beyond the description of either man. Upon its huge back rode three squat beast-men wielding heavy clubs.

It was evident that these savages were hostile by the way they brandished their weapons and called loudly in their guttural tongue.

"A fight's a fight wherever we are!" exclaimed Rens Karto. "If we're in Frejh, then by the Evil Gods who rule here, we'll take a few of her devils down the Long Passage with us!"

While Skortan hefted his enormous war-axe into his great hands, Karto whipped out his bright *Blood-Drinker*, his broadsword of fine steel and stood beside him.

The two still retaining their clubs leaped to the ground and made for Rens Karto. The third rode his mount full at Skortan who leaped aside and lashed at the monster with his horned head while his hands moved swift as a war-arrow hacking off the insect's long antennae with his axe. The beast-man, clinging to the monster's back, uttered a despairing cry. What Skortan had hoped for had happened. It writhed in terrible agony and within seconds it was dead. How unfortunate, reflected Skortan, that its rider was underneath it, crushed to death.

The Chieftain of Darsik turned towards Rens Karto to see if he needed any help. He was sitting on the ground nursing his wounds while one savage lay in his final death throes; the other was nowhere to be seen.

A few miles away, an airship had come to rest. Sojan and Nornos Rique were listening to the low moaning of primitive horns.

"Sounds like natives of some kind," said Sojan presently.

"There aren't any natives in this part of Poltoon," Nornos Rique argued. "Everybody knows that!"

"There weren't to my knowledge before I left Nornos Kad's court," replied Sojan, "but sometimes, recently, tales have come through about a nomad tribe of beast-men who seem to be heading slowly across the face of the continent."

"I'd like to find out what these wanderers are like," put in Andel. "What say we head in that direction?"

The party left the airship and headed north under the leadership of Sojan who knew the continent of Poltoon better than the rest. As they journeyed, the horns, weird and strange to the ears of Sojan and his friends grew louder and eerier until all at once they broke into a small clearing – crowded with savage beast-men.

Karto grinned weakly at his friend. "The other one escaped," he said, "that means he'll tell his friends, if he has any, and then – "

The weird savage music of the horns began to fill the air and suddenly the beast-men burst into the clearing.

The men didn't have a chance. Karto saw Skortan struggl-

ing underneath a mound of giant insects, then he felt a sharp pain in the back of his neck and saw no more.

As he awoke, the throbbing in his head gave place to the mournful hoot of the beast-men's horns. He was tied beside Skortan and the corpses of the dead were piled about them.

"It seems as if there's some kind of ceremony taking place," remarked Skortan, "if it's centred on us, as it undoubtedly is, I don't think it's going to be pleasant for us."

Suddenly the horns blew louder and the primitive men began to advance towards the two helpless companions. The largest raised a club and got ready to swing it down upon Rens Karto's outstretched body, intending to break the bones one by one. "You won't get any entertainment from me, damn you!" said Karto, closing his eyes and waiting for the first blow.

"By Yit!" yelled Sojan. "They've got a man there – and some kind of man-beast! Start shooting!" Frightened by the missiles which sped almost silently from the long-barrelled and powerful airguns, the beasts broke and fled.

Sojan rushed forward to free the two captives.

"Quick," he yelled, "before they get back!" The two friends did not understand the words but they could tell easily what he meant.

The party rushed into the forest and raced in the direction of the airship, Parijh leading the way.

Suddenly he swerved to the right. The rest automatically followed, for in front of them were scores of the beast-men.

"I can see a building over there!" shouted Parijh and ran towards it, not looking to see if the others were following. In a few minutes they were all safely inside.

Sojan glanced round. "This building is smaller, but very similar to the one we found in Shortani," he mused.

They crowded into a lift which, from past experience, they knew how to work.

Up they went to the third floor to find a huge room containing many strange machines.

In a corner a screen was glowing, blank like blind eyes it flickered occasionally but that was all.

Carefully Sojan studied the ancient script upon the dials and levers. While he bent over these controls his friends noted the little heaps of rubble, the odd piece of broken machinery here and there.

"It looks as if those natives somehow discovered how to get into this place," mused Nornos Rique. "And quite recently too. Probably some chance pressing of a button caused that screen to light up and scared them off."

"Very likely," said Sojan as he very deliberately pressed a stud. The screen faded, flickered, faded again and then an immense view of an alien landscape sprang into the frame.

Rens Karto and Skortan rushed towards it in wonder – for it was the home planet. The scene was one which was familiar to them and depicted the exact spot where they had been before being suddenly whisked to Zylor.

Frantically, by means of signs, the two conveyed this news to Sojan. Sojan was perplexed. How could two beings be on one planet one moment and on another the next?

"I just don't understand," he said, "no spaceship brought them, that's sure – but."

"I think I understand," said Nornos Rique. "This machinery may well have been used for transporting people from place to place without the aid of spaceships. How they did it I have not the remotest idea, but if they were capable of all the wonders we have seen recently, why not one more?"

"It smells of Dark Magic, to me," growled Andel.

"I also feel it is Evil," put in Parijh, "machinery I can understand – but this, no!"

"You're both a couple of superstitious barbarians still!" shouted Sojan.

"But if they got here – by Yet! then we'll get them back."

"How?" said Parijh simply, grinning a little into his short black beard.

"By readjusting the machine to what it was set at and thus break whatever is holding these two to Zylor!"

"Can you do it Sojan?" asked Nornos Rique quietly.

"I think so," replied the mercenary, "if you signal to these two to stand in the centre of that large machine over there, from what I've gleaned from the old writing, it will be an easy thing to send them back!"

By means of more signals they succeeded in placing the two Chieftains beneath a huge piece of machinery shaped like an inverted saucer. Then Sojan turned a switch. Abruptly the two men disappeared.

Jubilantly Sojan pointed to the screen. "Look!" he cried. "They're there already!"

And so they were, lying on the soft grass of Bersnol, a little dazed, a mile or two away from a large city.

"I'm glad that they are safe," said Sojan, "I feel that we have much in common with those two. We probably came from the same mother race who populated Zylor ages ago!"

"Very likely," said Nornos Rique. "Perhaps – one day – we shall meet them again!"

"Perhaps," said Sojan. "I hope so!"

(with Dick Ellingsworth)

J·CAWTHORN·76

ASPECTS OF
THE AUTHOR

No.1 THE APOCALYPTIC

THE SECRET LIFE OF ELRIC OF MELNIBONÉ
(1964)

Some years ago, when I was about eighteen, I wrote a novel called *The Golden Barge*. This was an allegorical fantasy about a little man completely without self-knowledge and with little of any other kind, going down a seemingly endless river, following a great Golden Barge which he felt, if he caught it would contain all truth, all secrets, all solutions to his problems. On the journey he met various groups of people, had a love affair, and so on. Yet every action he took in order to reach the Golden Barge seemed to keep him farther away from it. The river represented Time, the barge was what mankind is always seeking outside itself (when it can be found inside itself), etc., etc. The novel had a sad ending, as such novels do. Also, as was clear when I'd finished it, my handling of many of the scenes was clumsy and immature. So I scrapped it and decided that in future my allegories would be intrinsic within a conventional narrative – that the best symbols were the symbols found in familiar objects. Like swords for instance.

Up until I was twenty or so, I had a keen interest in fantasy fiction, particularly Sword & Sorcery stories of the kind written by Robert E. Howard, Clark Ashton Smith and the like, but this interest began to wane as I became more interested in less directly sensational forms of literature, just as earlier my interest in Edgar Rice Burroughs' tales had waned. I could still enjoy one or two Sword & Sorcery tales, particularly Poul Anderson's *The Broken Sword* and Fritz Leiber's *Grey Mouser* stories. A bit before this casting off of old loyalties, I had been in touch with Sprague De Camp and Hans Santessen of FANTASTIC UNIVERSE about doing a new series of Conan tales.

I think it was in the autumn of 1960, when I was working for SEXTON BLAKE LIBRARY and reading SF for SUSPENSE (the short-lived companion to ARGOSY) that I bumped into a colleague at Fleetway Publications, Andy Vincent, who was an old friend of Harry Harrison's (who had also freelanced for Fleetway for some time). Andy told me he was meeting Harry and Ted Carnell in the Fleetway foyer and suggested I went along. As I remember, that was where I first met Harry. Previously, I'd sold a couple of stories to Ted, one in collaboration with Barry Bayley, but had had more bounced than bought. Later on in a pub, Ted and I were talking about Robert E. Howard and Ted said he'd been thinking of running some Conan-type stuff in SCIENCE FANTASY. I told him of the FANTASTIC UNIVERSE idea which had fallen through when FANTASTIC UNIVERSE folded, and said I still had the stuff I'd done and would he like to see it. He said he would. A couple of days later I sent him the first chapter and outline of a Conan story. To tell you the truth, writing in Howard's style had its limitations, as did his hero as far as I was concerned, and I wasn't looking forward to producing another 10,000 words of the story if Ted liked it.

Ted liked it – or at least he liked the writing, but there had been a misunderstanding. He hadn't wanted Conan – he had wanted something on the same lines.

This suited me much better. I decided that I would think up a hero as different as possible from the usual run of S-and-S heroes, and use the narrative as a vehicle for my own 'serious' ideas. Many of these ideas, I realise now, were somewhat romantic and coloured by a long drawn-out and, to me at the time, tragic love affair which hadn't quite finished its course and which was confusing and darkening my outlook. I was writing floods of hack work for Fleetway and was getting sometimes £70 or £80 a week which was going on drink, mainly, and, as I remember, involved rather a lot of broken glass of one description or another. I do remember, with great pride, my main achievement of the winter of 1960 or 1961, which was to smash entirely an unbreakable plate-glass door in a well-known restaurant near Piccadilly. And the management apologised. . . .

I'm mentioning this, to give a picture of my mood at the time of Elric's creation. If you've read the early Elric stories in particular, you'll see that Elric's outlook was rather similar to mine. My point is, that Elric *was* me (the me of 1960–1, anyway) and the mingled qualities of betrayer and betrayed, the bewilderment about life in general, the search for some solution to it all, the expression of this bewilderment in terms of violence, cynicism and the need for revenge, were all characteristics of mine. So when I got the chance to write *The Dreaming City*, I was identifying very closely with my hero-villain. I thought myself something of an outcast (another romantic notion largely unsubstantiated now I look back) and emphasised Elric's physical differences accordingly :

> His bizarre dress was tasteless and gaudy, and did not match his sensitive face and long-fingered, almost delicate hands, yet he flaunted it since it emphasised that he did not belong in any company – that he was an outsider and an outcast. But, in reality, he had little need to wear such outlandish gear – for . . . (he) was a pure albino who drew his power from a secret and terrible source.
>
> (*Stealer of Souls*, page 13)

The story was packed with personal symbols (as are all the stories bar a couple). The 'secret and terrible source' was the sword *Stormbringer*, which symbolised my own and others tendency to rely on mental and physical crutches rather than cure the weakness at source. To go further, Elric, for me, symbolised the ambivalence of mankind in general, with its love-hates, its mean-generosity, its confident-bewilderment act. Elric is a thief who believes *himself* robbed, a lover who hates love. In short, he cannot be sure of the truth of anything, not even of his own emotions or ambitions. This is made much clearer in a story containing even more direct allegory, the second in the series, *While the Gods Laugh*. Unfortunately, Ted left out the verse from which the title was taken:

> I, while the gods laugh, the world's vortex am;
> Maelstrom of passions in that hidden sea,
> Whose waves of all-time lap the coasts of me,
> And in small compass the dark waters cram.
>
> Mervyn Peake (*Shapes and Sounds*)

This, I think, gave more meaning to both title and story which involved a long quest after the Dead God's Book – a mythical work alleged to contain all the knowledge of the universe, in which Elric feels, he will at last find the true meaning of life. He expresses this need in a somewhat rhetorical way. When the wingless woman Shaarilla asks him why he wants the book he replies:

"I desire, if you like, to know one of (misprinted as *or* in magazine version) two things. Does an ultimate God exist or not? Does Law or Chaos govern our lives? Man needs a God, so the philosophers tell us. Have they made one – or did one make them?" etc., etc.

Here, as in other passages, the bewilderment is expressed in metaphysical terms, for at that time, due mainly to my education I was very involved with mysticism. Also, the metaphysical terms suited the description of a Sword-and-Sorcery hero and his magical, low-technology world.

It may seem odd that I use such phrases as 'at that time' and so on, as if I'm referring to the remote past, but in many ways, being a trifle more mature, perhaps, happily married with a better sense of direction, etc., all this *does* seem to have taken place in the remote past.

The Dead God's Book is eventually located in a vast underground world which I had intended as a womb-symbol, and after a philosophical conversation with the book's keeper, Elric discovers it. This passage is, to me now, rather overwritten, but, for better or worse :

> It was a huge book – the Dead God's Book, its covers encrusted with alien gems from which the light sprang. It gleamed, it *throbbed* with light and brilliant colour.
> "At last," Elric breathed. "At last – the truth!"
> He stumbled forward like a man made stupid with drink, his pale hands reaching for the thing he sought with such savage bitterness. His hands touched the pulsating cover of the Book and, trembling, turned it back. . . . With a crash, the cover fell to the floor, sending the bright gems skipping and dancing over the paving stone. *Beneath Elric's . . . hands lay nothing but a pile of yellowish dust.*

The Dead God's Book and the Golden Barge are one and the same. They have no real existence, save in the wishful imagination of mankind. There is, the story says, no Holy Grail which will transform a man overnight from bewildered ignorance to complete knowledge – the answer already is within him, if he cares to train himself to find it. A rather over-emphasised fact, throughout history, but one generally ignored all the same.

The Stealer of Souls, the third story, continues this theme, but brought in rather different kinds of symbols. Coupled with the Jungarian symbols already inherent in any tale using direct mythic material, I used Freudian symbols, too. This was a cynical attempt and a rather vulgar attempt to make the series popular. It appeared to work. *The Stealer of Souls*, whatever else it may be, is one of the most pornographic stories I have ever written. In Freudian terms it is the description of, if you like, a night's love-making.

Which brings me to another point. Although there is comparatively little direct description of sexual encounters in the stories and what there are are largely romanticised, the whole

Elric saga has, in its choice of situations and symbols, very heavy sexual undertones. This is true of most Sword-and-Sorcery stories, but I have an idea that I may be the first such author to understand his material to this extent, to know what he's using. If I hadn't been a bit fed-up by the big response received by *The Stealer of Souls* (magazine story, not the book) I could have made even greater use of what I discovered.

Other critics have pointed out the close relationship the horror story (and often the SF story for that matter) has with the pornographic story, so there's no need to go any deeper into it here.

The pornographic content of the Elric saga doesn't interest me much, but I have hinted at the relationship between sex and violence in several places, and, indeed, there are a dozen syndromes to be found in the stories, particularly if you bear in mind my own involvement with sexual love, expression in violence, etc., at the time the stories were first conceived. Even my own interpretation of what I was doing is open to interpretation, in this case!

The allegory goes through all ten stories (including *To Rescue Tanelorn* which did not feature Elric) in SCIENCE FANTASY, but it tends to change its emphasis as my own ideas take better shape and my emotions mature. When, in the last Elric story of all, the sword, his crutch, *Stormbringer* turns and slays Elric it is meant to represent, on one level, how mankind's wish-fantasies can often bring about the destruction of (till now at least) part of mankind. Hitler, for instance, found his whole so-called 'political' creed on a series of wish-fantasies (this is detailed in that odd book *Dawn of Magic*, recently published here). Again this is an old question, a bit trite from being asked too often, maybe, but how much of what we believe *is* true and how much is what we *wish* were true. Hitler dreamed of his Thousand Year Reich, Chamberlain said There Will Be No War. Both were convinced – both ignored plain fact to a frightening extent, just as many people (not just politicians whose public statements are not always what they really believe) ignore plain facts today. This is no

new discovery of mine. It is probably one of the oldest dis-
coveries in the world. But, in part, this is what nearly all my
published work points out. Working, as I did once, as editor
of a party journal (allegedly an information magazine for
party candidates) this conviction was strengthened. The build-
up of a fantasy is an odd process and sometimes happens, to
digress a bit, like this.

The facts are gathered, related, a picture emerges. The
picture, though slightly coloured by the personalities of the
fact-relaters, is fairly true. The picture is given to the politician.
If the politician is a man of integrity he will not deliberately
warp the facts, but he will present them in a simplified
version which will be understood by the general public (he
thinks). This involves a selection, which can change a picture
out of all recognition, though the politician didn't deliberately
intend to warp the facts. The other kind of politician almost
automatically selects and warps in order to prove a point he,
or his party, is trying to make. So the fantasy begins, until
quite often, facts are built on fantasy, until the real picture is
almost irrevocably lost.

Therefore this reliance on pseudo-knowledge which seems to
prove something we wish were true, is a dangerous thing to do.

This is one of the main messages of the Elric series, though
there are several others on different levels.

Don't think I'm asking you to go back over the stories
looking for these allegories and symbols. The reason I aban-
doned *The Golden Barge* was because among other things it
wasn't entertaining. The Elric stories are meant to entertain
as much as anything else, but if anyone cares to look for
substance beyond the entertainment level, they might find it.

One of the main reasons, though, for taking this angle when
Alan (Dodd) asked me to write a piece on Elric, was because I
have been a little disappointed at the first book being dis-
missed by some professional critics (who evidently didn't
bother to read it closely, if at all) as an imitation of Conan.
When you put thought and feeling into a story – thought and
feeling which is yours – you don't much care for being called

an imitator or a plagiarist however good or bad the story. Probably the millionth novel about a young advertising executive in love with a deb and involved with a married woman has just been published, yet the author won't be accused of imitating anyone or plagiarising anyone. It is the use to which one puts one's chosen material, not that material, which matters.

FOR ten thousand years the sorcerer-kings of melnibone ruled the earth.

ten thousand years of a forgotten age, serving the realm of Chaos, while the new creature, man, grew in their shadow. And then melnibone fell, thrown down amid monstrous wars, shattered by frightful ruins. Chaos and law clashed, striving for mastery of the cosmos, and the earth shook.

It was a time of destiny for men and gods, a time of heroes. Chief among these was ELRIC, last emperor of melnibone, lord of dragons. ELRIC, who had destroyed his homeland in revenge for the death of his sister and lover, Cymoril. ELRIC, a crimson-eyed albino who drew his strength from a black blade which drank the souls of its victims....

STORMBRINGER

ONLY the island of melnibone remained untouched by Chaos. mounted on dragons, ELRIC, his friend moonglum of elwher, and his kinsman dyvim slorm, rose from the ruins of imrryr, the dreaming city, to their final battle with the chaos hordes. only ELRIC could summon the lords of law to fight for Earth, but his life was slowly ebbing....

ELRIC
(1963)

Very nice of you to devote so much time to Elric – though he doesn't altogether merit it! I'd disagree with the writer when he says, "I expect the 'sword and sorcery' stories are by far the most popular type . . . etc." I think those who like them receive them enthusiastically, but it's a fairly small minority compared with those who like, for instance, 'science fantasy' of *The Dragon Masters* variety and the stuff Kuttner, Brackett and others used to turn out for STARTLING, SUPER SCIENCE, etc. These days people seem to want information of some kind with their escapism – and 'sword and sorcery' doesn't strictly supply information of the type required. (The appeal of James Bond appears to be based primarily on the lumps of pseudo-data inserted every so often in the narrative). The only 'sword and sorcery' stuff I personally enjoy reading is Leiber's. Don't go much for Tolkein, Dunsany, Smith, Howard – or Edgar Rice Burroughs in spite of what some critics have said of my books recently.

Though I didn't know SCIENCE FANTASY was due to fold when I wrote it, I wound up the Elric series just in time to catch the last issue quite by coincidence. I had intended to kill off Elric (as is probably plain from the second story in the currently appearing quartette, *Black Sword's Brothers*) and his world, so it is just as well. A story set in a world which so closely borders Elric's that some of the place names are the same will be appearing in FANTASTIC some time this year. This was originally called *Earl Aubec and the Golem* but the title has

been changed to *Master of Choas* (the cosmology is iden-
tical with the Elric stories cosmology) and will be, if Cele
Goldsmith likes the next one I'm planning, the first of a series
showing the development of the Earth from a rather unusual
start. It is vaguely possible that Elric will appear in future
stories and some of his background not filled in in the conclud-
ing stories (*Sad Giant's Shield* in SCIENCE FANTASY No 63 and
Doomed Lord's Passing in SCIENCE FICTON 64) will be filled in
there. But this depends on how the series develops and what
Cele Goldsmith thinks of the stories. *Masters of Chaos* is, I
think, in many ways my best S & S tale.

It is a great disappointment, however, that SCIENCE
FANTASY has folded. Not simply because stories sold to it paid
my rent, but because for me and many other writers in this
country (particularly, like me, the younger ones) it was an
outlet for the kind of story that is very difficult to sell in
America – even to Cele Goldsmith who appears to be the
most open-minded of the U.S. editors. Particularly this went
for the short novel of the *Earth is But a Star* length and the
recent 37,000 word *Skeleton Crew* by Aldiss. The slow developing, borderline-mainstream story of the kind Ballard does so
well will find more difficulty selling in the states too, though
Ballard's *Question of Re-entry* was of this kind and published
in FANTASTIC. It seems a pity that English SF has reached, in
people like Ballard and Aldiss, an exceptionally high standard
and a strongly English flavour, and now has no markets here.

The landscapes of my stories are metaphysical, not physical.
As a faltering atheist with a deep irradicable religious sense (I
was brought up on an off-beat brand of Christian Mysticism)
I tended, particularly in the early stories like *While the God's
Laugh*, to work out my own problems through Elric's adventures. Needless to say, I never reached any conclusions, merely
brought these problems closer to the surface. I was writing
not particularly well, but from the 'soul'. I wasn't just telling
a story, I was telling *my* story. I don't think of myself as a
fantasy writer in the strict sense – but the possibilities of fantasy
attract me. For some sort of guide to what I see as worth

exploiting in the fantasy form, I'd suggest you bear this in mind when you read *The Deep Fix* which will appear in the last issue of SCIENCE FANTASY along with *Dead God's Passing*, the last Elric story . . . which might also provide a clue. *Deep Fix* will be under a pseudonym (the late James Colvin, ed.).

I am not a logical thinker. I am, if anything, an intuitive thinker. Most facts bore me. Some inspire me. Nuclear physics, for instance, though I know scarcely anything about the field, excites me, particularly when watching a nuclear physicist explaining his theories on TV. My only interest in any field of knowledge is literary. This is probably a narrow interest, but I'm a writer and want to be a good one. I have only written two fantasy stories in my life which were deliberately commercial (sorry, three – one hasn't been published). These were *Going Home* in SCIENCE FICTION ADVENTURES and *Kings in Darkness* in SCIENCE FANTASY. The rest, for better or worse, were written from inside. Briefly, physics doesn't interest me – metaphysics does. The only writer of SF I enjoy is J. G. Ballard. The only writer of fantasy currently working in the magazines I like is Leiber. The three works of fantasy I can still re-read and enjoy, apart from those, are Anderson's *The Broken Sword*, Peake's Titus Groan trilogy, and Cabell's *Jurgen*. Anderson has done nothing better than *The Broken Sword*, in my opinion, and I sometimes feel that his talent has since been diverted, even lessened. I feel that writing SF can ruin and bleed dry a writer's talent. The best he can do in this field is improve his technique – at the expense of his art. I think of myself as a bad writer with big ideas, but I'd rather be that than a big writer with bad ideas – or ideas that have gone bad. I tend to think of the SF magazine field as a field in which it is possible to experiment – and sell one's mistakes; but the impulse to sell tends to dominate the impulse to experiment the longer one stays in the field.

And fear of death, incidentally, is probably another source of inspiration in the Elric stories. I don't believe in life after death and I don't want to die. I hope I shan't. Maybe I'll be the exception that proves the rule. . . .

Now for some specific remarks about the Elric material in 'Niekas'. Firstly, a few carping points on the spelling. As you'll see from the book *Stealer of Souls*, which I had an opportunity to get at before it was printed, there an accented é in the spelling of Melniboné. Melnibonay – this accent was, of course, left out of all but the first story. Imrryr is spelt thus. Count Smiorgan Baldhead – not *of* Baldhead (his head was hairless).

A point about the end of *The Dreaming City*. Elric used the wind to save himself, abandoning his comrades to the dragons. This, and Cymoril's death, is on his conscience.

I don't know whether the Imrryians would have *despised* Elric (second story synopsis, line 1). I think of them as accepting his treachery fairly calmly, and yet bound to do something about it if they caught up with him.

When I wrote this story I was thinking of Stormbringer as a symbol – partly, anyway – of Man's reliance on mental and physical crutches he'd be better off without. It seems a bit pretentious, now. I suppose you could call the Dharzi zombie men, but really I didn't think of them as men at all, in the strict sense. The sea is, of course, an underground sea – and also not 'natural' as Elric discovered. The hill, castle, etc. – all the bits and pieces in this episode – are all underground. There was the intention here to give the whole episode the aspect of taking place within a womb. The book is a similar symbol to the sword in this story. Again, in the end of this story, he leaves Shaarilla to her fate – abandoning her. At this period of my writing women either got killed or had some other dirty trick played on them. The only female character who survived was my own La Belle Dame Sans Merci – Yishana. I won't explain here – too personal. . . .

"The exact nature of the feud is a mystery" (*Theleb K'aarna*, line 6). Maybe it wasn't clear enough here – but I have the idea that I explained somewhere how Theleb K'aarna had devised a means of sending Elric on a wild-goose chase by loosing some supernatural force or other against him. This was why Elric wanted blood. That story by the way was the most popular of the first three. I guess a Freudian psychologist would know why. . . .

Kings in Darkness I'd rather not deal with, since it was the worst of the series and, as I mentioned, written commercially. Therefore there is little of it which fits in with what I like to to think of as the *real* content of the Elric series.

No comments, either, on *The Flame Bringers* – although I enjoyed writing the Meerclar bit and the last sequence with Elric on the back of the dragon. This, I think, is nothing much more than an adventure story, though it serves to show up Elric's weakness in that the moment things get tough he's seeking his sword again. Also the last bit where the sword returns is a hint of the sword's 'true' nature.

In the book version of the last quartette (of which *Black Sword's Brothers* is the first part) I've revised the opening a bit. It was – and C. R. Kearns pointed this out and I agreed with him – what you might call a confused start. In the final revision of the short story version I changed it fairly considerably from the original and one or two inconsistencies crept through – I was working hard at the time and was very tired.

I would rather you had left this story out or waited until all four had been published before synopsising it since this is the first part of a novel and many issues are not clarified until the end. I'm not happy with any of the magazine stories as they stand and have made, in places, quite heavy revisions. The last story to be written is, I feel, the best though. A final word – the Lords of Chaos hated Tanelorn not because it was a utopia, but because nearly all those in the city had once owed them, the Lords, allegiance and had foresworn it when they came to Tanelorn (or so the story goes). This is probably the most overtly philosophical or mystical of the Young Kingdom tales, as you say, and took much longer to write than the rest. It could be improved, I feel, by more play on the actual characters involved.

The writer feels that *Black Sword's Brothers* was the dullest Elric story. It was certainly, as explained above, one of the most patchy from the point of view of construction. It's true, in one sense, that I was losing interest in the Elric series – or rather that I had reached a point before it was written where I had run out of inspiration. But the interest picked up as I began to write and, by the time I'd got into the second part, I was enjoying the writing again. I think it's possible to look at the Elric stories as a sort of presentation of the crude materials which I hope to fashion into better stories later. Being non-logical, I have to produce a great deal of stuff in order to find the bits of it I really want. My ideas about Law and Chaos and the rest became clearer as I wrote. Of the four, *Black Sword's Brothers* and *Sad Giant's Shield* (the most recently published) are the weakest in my opinion. Both were revised (something I do not usually do with the Elric stories) and both suffered from this revision, I think. My mind was at its clearest (not very clear by normal standards) when I wrote *Doomed Lord's Passing*. I've found that I can only really learn from my mistakes after they've been published, which is hard on the reader.

Ted Carnell, who handles my other work as well, said that he felt *Earl Aubec and the Golem* (or *Master of Chaos*) was a sort of crystallisation of everything I'd been working on in the Elric series. Maybe not everything, but I think he's right. Earl Aubec is more a kind of sword-and-philosophy tale than an outright sword-and-sorcery. Elric tales – or the best of them – were conceived similarly.

The writer thinks the John Rackham's fantasies (or properly 'Occult-thrillers') will outlast my stories. I don't think either will last for long, but I might as well admit that I was slightly hurt by this remark, for Rackham's stories that I have read struck me as being rather barren, stereotyped tales with no 'true' sense of the occult at all (whatever a true sense of the occult is). Moreover I know John doesn't believe in his stuff for a second (at least not in any supernatural sense) whereas I believe wholeheartedly in mine, as I've pointed out. It's silly to take up someone's remark like this, especially since it is fair criticism and just a statement of someone's individual taste, but I suppose I'm still young enough to feel defensive about my stories – especially my Elric stories for which I have an odd mixture of love and hate. They are so closely linked to my own obsessions and problems that I find it hard to ignore any criticisms of them and tend momentarily to leap to their defence.

As I said earlier, and Cele Goldsmith said in a supplement to AMRA, sword-and-sorcery seems to appeal to an enthusiastic minority and may receive a large volume of praise from a fairly small section of readers.

When Carnell asked me to think up a sword-and-sorcery series I tried to make it as different as possible from any other I'd read. I'd hesitate to agree that the two best known magic swords are Excalibur and Prince Valiant's 'Singing Blade' – Excalibur, certainly, and probably Roland's Durandala. The idea of the magic sword came, of course, from legend, but I willingly admit to Anderson's influence, too. The idea of an albino hero had a more obscure source. As a boy I collected a pre-war magazine called UNION JACK. This was Sexton Blake's Own Paper – Blake was the British version of your Nick Carter, I should imagine, and UNION JACK was the equivalent of your Dime Novels. One of Blake's most memorable opponents was a character named M. Zenith – or Zenith the Albino, a Byronic hero-villain who aroused more sympathy in the reader than did the intrepid detective. Anyway, the Byronic h-v had always appealed; I liked the idea of an albino, which suited my purpose, and so Elric was born – an albino. Influences include various Gothic novels, also. Elric is not a new hero to fantasy – although he's new, I suppose, to S-and-S.

I cannot altogether agree that Elric remains an essentially simple character. I think of him as complex, but inarticulate when he tries to explain his predicament. His taste for revenge seems to be a sort of extension of his search for peace and purpose – he finds, to coin a phrase, forgetfulness in action. Elric's guilt over the slaying of Nikora was guilt for the *slaying* itself, not because he'd killed a particular man.

I don't know whether I could have left Moonglum out and still kept the stories the same. Moonglum is, apart from everything else, to some extent a close, valued friend of mine who has been a lot of help in various ways over the last few years. If Elric is my fantasy self, then Moonglum is this friend's fantasy self (as I see him at any rate). I am not particularly gloomy by nature. I put Moonglum in to make remarks about Elric when he gets too self-absorbed or too absorbed in self-pity, etc.

A little more of Elric's background and some clue as to why he is what he is will be found in *Dead God's Passing*. I've been aware of this absence and have tried to rectify it a bit here.

I was pleased that you have used the *Grey Mouser* as comparison since, as must now be evident, I'm a great fan of the Mouser's. Perhaps Moonglum also owes a little to the Mouser. As for Elric being an idealist rather than a materialist, this is probably because I'm often told I'm a materialist rather than an idealist. I don't like to be told this, but it could be true.

Elric's disregard for danger is of the nature of panic rather than courage, maybe. The Mouser, on the other hand, seems not to disregard danger – he evaluates it then acts. Conan – well. . . .

The cosmology of the Elric stories probably owes its original inspiration to two things – Zoroastrianism (which I admire) and Anderson's *Three Hearts and Three Lions*. It was developed from there, of course. This set-up simply is :

COSMIC HAND
"
"
"
"

Balance
Law   Chaos
Grey Lords
Elementals
Men
Beasts

Law Sorcerers   Chaos Sorcerers
Men pledged to Law   Men pledged to Chaos

I have a more complex chart. The sixth story is the one where the cosmology becomes clearer and the reader should realise the rest as he reads the last stories.

I have probably helped anyone who wants to assess the Elric stories on a slightly different level. Who wants to?

J·CAWTHORN·76

ASPECTS OF THE AUTHOR

No.2 THE AESTHETIC

NEW WORLDS —
JERRY CORNELIUS
(1972)

New worlds began as a magazine founded by SF enthusiasts in the middle 1940s. A consortium published the first few issues. This consortium consisted of, among others, Bill Temple, Ted Carnell, Leslie Flood, John Wyndham, Frank Arnold and Steve Frances. Later Maclarens took it over (though the company remained independent as Nova Publications Ltd.), and published it for the best part of its career with Ted Carnell as editor. Ted published the first Ballard stories and the work of then-starting authors like Brunner, Aldiss, Roberts, etc. In 1964 the circulations of the magazines (SCIENCE FANTASY was also edited by Ted) were very low and Maclarens decided to fold the titles. David Warburton of Roberts and Vinter Ltd., heard they were folding and decided to buy them. Ted wanted to edit his new anthology series, NEW WRITINGS IN SF, and so recommended me as editor. Warburton wanted two editors (wisely), one for each of the magazines. I chose NEW WORLDS and Kyril Bonfiglioli became editor of SCIENCE FANTASY. My first issue, in a paperback-style format, but a magazine in all other respects, appeared for May–June 1964 (number 142). We ran as a bi-monthly for a short time and then went monthly with issue 146. Many people expected me to opt for the editorship of SCIENCE FANTASY, since most of my work had previously appeared in that magazine, but in fact I was interested in broadening the possibilities of the SF idiom and NEW WORLDS, being a much more open title, seemed the best place to do it. My first editorial stated pretty much the policy I have followed ever since, though perhaps I'm a little more sophisticated now. Also I was naïve in thinking there were a lot of authors who shared the sense of frustration which Ballard and I had felt for some years. I tried to find good young authors and follow what one might call a policy of enlightened conservatism – publishing the best of the old and the best of the new. There were a lot of outcries when we started dealing with explicit sex (never an important issue to us) and so on, also when the first Ballard fragmented narratives began to appear with *The Atrocity Exhibition*, also with the rather astringent criticism of 'Golden Age' masters of SF, etc., but gradually readers began to realise that there was value in the new stuff and it didn't take long before they were criticising the newer stuff in its own terms. We *were* crusading but we weren't thinking in terms of tabu-breaking and so on, because the restrictions here had never been as marked as they were in the U.S. We were seriously attempting to find new ways of dealing with new subject matter and we always placed substance before style. People have since confused our 'revolution' with a stylistic revolution, but our principal aim was concerned with substance and structure – it had little to do with what Judy Merril and Harlan Ellison, for instance, later came to term the 'new wave' in U.S. SF. We were specifically out to perpetuate, if you like, the European moral tradition in literature. We hardly 'rejected' the U.S. pulp tradition, because it had never much influenced us anyway. Some of the writers, indeed, were quite conservative in their tastes and styles – Disch, for instance, who became closely associated with the magazine (and still is). While having no prejudice against it (and admiring much of it) we had little in common with the aims apparently represented in the work of the newer (or regenerated) U.S. writers like Ellison, Delany, Zelazny, Lafferty or Silverberg. We also, of course, published most of those writers at some stage, and were pleased to do so, because we always strove for a broad representation of the best work of its kind. I feel we published some of the best work done by them – Zelazny's *For A Breath I Tarry* (later reprinted, I think, in AMAZING) and several others: Ellison's *Boy and His Dog*, Delany's *Time Considered as a Helix*, etc. But our main *raison d'être* became the publishing of what some would call 'experimental' work and when, in 1967, Roberts and Vinter suffered severe financial set-backs (not over the SF magazines), Brian Aldiss was responsible for suggesting to the Arts Council (responsible for encouraging and maintaining the arts; a government-financed agency) that they help us. Thanks largely to the enthusiasm of Angus Wilson, then chairman of the Council, and letters from various distinguished critics and academics (rallied by Brian) we received an award which, while not enough to support us in any way – save as a 'little magazine' – gave us the moral support we needed and I became part-publisher, putting my own money into the magazine and going to the large, 'glossy' format we then adopted. Unfortunately the two business partners I had to begin with showed themselves over-cautious and pulled out so that the magazine schedules were thrown into confusion. During 1967–8 we followed an erratic schedule culminating in the banning of two issues by the two major British distributors and the banning of the magazine in South Africa, New Zealand, Australia, etc. All of these areas were fairly crucial to us and if it hadn't been for advertising we should have had to fold. Also the newspapers came out in our favour and the ban was technically lifted. It was at this time that a Question was asked in the House of Commons about public money being spent on a 'pornographic' magazine and it seemed for a while that we would lose the grant. This blew over and I became sole publisher of the magazine. Foolishly, I didn't form a company to publish the magazine, so that I became personally responsible for the debts. From 1968 to 1971 I published NEW WORLDS. In 1970 it emerged that the distributors had been receiving large quantities of NEW WORLDS and had deliberately refrained from distributing them without telling us because they wanted to avoid any further newspaper publicity. Effectively we lost the income on six months' issues and I suddenly found myself owing over £3000, which I didn't have. This was at a time when, thanks particularly to Charles Platt who was editing the magazine and running the business affairs, NEW WORLDS had become viable. I was forced to wind NEW WORLDS up, publishing a last 'Subscription Only' issue (No. 201) in 1971, as an independent company. Tom Dardis of Berkley expressed an interest in doing NEW WORLDS as a Quarterly and Anthony Cheetham was very enthusiastic about doing it through Sphere in this country, so I did four issues for Berkley who then decided that sales didn't merit their continuing the series. I decided, though the Sphere sales were on the increase, to cut back to two issues a year for the time being, since the Sphere advance alone wasn't sufficient to cover what I wanted to do and we're still partially financing the British editions through subsidiary income derived, for instance, from my editing fees for the *Best of New Worlds* series and so on. And, of course, I'm still paying off the creditors for the large size issues.

The daily routine? It varied, depending on who was publishing the magazine or, for that matter, who was editing it, since I didn't, of course, edit it for the whole time. The early days were fairly quiet, with just Lang Jones and myself doing the whole thing from an office I had in Southwark. Later I began to work from home, going into the publisher's office about once a week, and later still Charles Platt joined the staff as art editor and much improved the appearance of the paperback size issues. That period, too, was the only time I was actually getting paid to do it! By and large I tend to set one or two days a week aside for reading. Lang Jones is our best copy-editor and he would tend to do that (and still does) after I'd done the rough copy-editing. We never change stories without consultation with the author and the author's viewpoint is always respected. Where we have changes to suggest we tend to Xerox the manuscript, make the suggestions on the Xerox and send them to the author for his or her comments. If the author disagrees we'll discuss alternatives until we're both satisfied. This extends even to titles. The office always ran on democratic lines, with every editor being encouraged to encourage authors who suited his particular taste. This meant, of course, that I'd sometimes publish stories I couldn't stand or that I would include stories others didn't like, but we reached a fairly satisfactory compromise ("I'll put this story in I think is brilliant because you're putting in that story *you* think is brilliant"). I don't believe there's such a thing as objective literary judgement for someone running a magazine and it seemed the best way of ensuring the representation of as many different kinds of writing as possible. The special 'New Writers' issues we have done have largely been the work of people like Jim Sallis, Graham Hall, Mike Harrison, Graham Charnock and Charles Platt. Through most of the magazine's career there was always something of a 'commune' feel about the day-to-day editing, with authors and staff getting together to discuss specific stories or general policy. The issues about which I am happiest, I suppose, are the first few of the 1967–8 large size issues where my own policies found their strongest expression. To me, these were the best issues – say from 173 to 176 where we got a good balance between science and art features, artwork, good 'conventional' fiction and good 'experimental' fiction. Particular issues came after that which I particularly liked but not as a 'run'. I enjoyed doing the special 201st issue (labelled our Special Good Taste Issue and containing a distinctly Victorian feel!). The last thing I can think of to say about the day-to-day running of the magazine was that it filled the minds of a fairly large group of us for a long time -- i.e. social life for many of us was centred around the magazine. It dominated our days. A rather heady and hectic love affair in which the magazine could be seen from time to time as either an inspiring mistress or a vampiric femme fatale. Certainly the publishing problems dominated my days and nights for several years.

I think we accomplished a fair amount. Without doubt we altered the attitudes of many publishers towards the newer ideas we were promoting. We encouraged many authors to do their best and/or most interesting work. Many authors, for instance, claimed that without NEW WORLDS they would have given up writing or that they would have become cynical about their writing or that they wouldn't have put so much work into something. Aldiss, Ballard, Disch, Sladek, Roberts and others have all said, at different times, that NEW WORLDS encouraged them to do their best work. We were responsible for interesting many critics, academics and journalists in what might be called the SF renaissance. I think we achieved an enormous amount. If what we were trying to do has been misinterpreted in America this has largely been because most people received their impressions at second hand through, say, the Judith Merril YEAR'S BEST and ENGLAND SWINGS anthologies. Judy did a lot to publicise NEW WORLDS and was a good friend, but her interpretations were often somewhat at odds with our views! NEW WORLDS became a banner in Judy's own crusade – and Judy, after all, started the ball rolling in the U.S. If the issues became clouded in rhetoric about 'new wave speculative fiction' or 'The New Thing', it wasn't much to do with us. Harlan Ellison followed Judy with DANGEROUS VISIONS and I think it's fair to claim that again, if obliquely, NEW WORLDS supplied the impetus. I think, however, that battles are being fought in the States which have been over in this country for some years – everyone's settled down to doing their own thing. There was never any danger of one idea superceding another but it was necessary to make room for other ideas and that, if nothing else, is what NEW WORLDS achieved. And our influence, if that isn't too pompous a phrase, extended well beyond the SF world in this country, if nowhere else. We know many rock musicians who've claimed that NEW WORLDS gave them the impetus they were looking for, for we know artists, non-SF writers and poets who think the same. A lot of our ideas – and, indeed, our contributors – turned up in the pages of the 'alternative' press. We still meet readers of the large size NEW WORLDS who tell us it was the only magazine which gave them any hope or spoke to them in a vocabulary which made sense to them. And we have possibly influenced the vocabulary (both in terms of ideas and language) of SF – broadened its possiblities. Failures?

SOJAN

We claimed too much for what we were doing in the early days and are only now beginning to see the results. We never licked the distribution problem – until it was too late – and so never reached as many readers as we might have done. We failed completely to convince the majority of fans that we felt writers like Heinlein were short-changing them with bad writing and simple-minded notions. We failed to improve the standard of writing in SF, which, in the main, remains abominable. On the other hand we offered an alternative to readers who couldn't face that kind of writing and, of course, we still do. We've certainly failed to convince the majority of U.S. publishers concerning the merits of typical NEW WORLDS fiction for they plainly prefer to publish the sensationalistic and poorly-conceived SF they have always published – and their preference doesn't appear to be dictated by commercial reasoning. We've failed, perhaps, to produce a large market for the kind of fiction we like best, but we have produced a large enough one to make publishing that fiction a viable proposition (which it wasn't, even five years ago). And, by and large, we've failed to get across to most SF fans the seriousness of our intentions, the purpose of our intentions. This again, perhaps, is because our particular point of view has been obscured by interpreters. Certainly NEW WORLDS' policy has little to do with what most U.S. fans would identify as the 'SF New Wave'.

Which, I suppose, almost brings us to Jerry Cornelius.

Jerry Cornelius began as a version of Elric of Melniboné when, in late 1964, I was casting around for a means of dealing with what I regarded as the 'hot' subject matter of my own time – stuff associated with scientific advance, social change, the mythology of the mid-twentieth century. Since Elric was a 'myth' character I decided to try to write his first stories in twentieth century terms. *The Final Programme* was written, in first draft, in about ten days in January 1965. It began as a kind of rewrite of the first two Elric stories, *The Dreaming City* and *While the Gods Laugh*. By doing this I found a style and a form which most suited what I wanted to write about. I was elated. I borrowed as much from the Hammett school of thriller fiction as I borrowed from SF and I think I found my own 'voice' as a writer. Influences included Ronald Firbank and, to a minor extent, William Burroughs (two not dissimilar figures in my estimation). I felt, at the time, that I had at last found a way of marrying 'serious' fiction with 'popular' fiction and I had always believed that science fiction was the form which could most easily act, as it were, as the ideal environment in which this marriage could take place. (This, incidentally, was the idea which was behind much of the NEW WORLDS policy). SF knew how to cope with much of the subject matter and was a vital and popular form but was largely unable to deal with the traditional and sophisticated moral questions found in the best fiction, largely because its accepted forms had denied any attempt authors might make to incorporate these questions – the form as it stood distorted and simplified the problems. Just as Ballard found his remedy in the form he used for *Atrocity Exhibition* and the later stories published from 1965 onwards, I felt I'd found my remedy in the form I used in *The Final Programme* – by using a character who *accepted* the moral questions without discussing them (the dialogue tends to take for granted the reader's familiarity with the questions and doesn't detail them – doesn't spell them out) and by supplying the reader with a straightforward dynamic narrative which he could enjoy for its own sake. The plot, while being unimportant, was supplied for those who required a plot to keep them reading. Moreover, I prefer, in the main, books with a straightforward plot, too, so I was trying to produce something I'd enjoy reading. I was very pleased with the book and thought that everyone else would enjoy it, too, if only for its ironies and sensations. A couple of British publishers asked to see it and surprised me with their strong reactions – I'd written the book to shock, they said, and I wouldn't get anywhere like that. It hadn't occurred to me

that the book would do anything but amuse (if nothing else).
I despaired, became cynical, put the book aside. A copy went
out automatically to my, then, agents, Scott Meredith. In
1967 the book was bought, enthusiastically, by George Ernsberger, then an editor at Avon. Parts of it had been published
in NEW WORLDS in 1965 and 1966 as an experiment in cutting
up chunks and putting them in a different order (a mistake,
I now think). By this time I had begun what was eventually
published as *A Cure For Cancer*. I had started the book using
another character's name and hadn't got very far when I
realised that this was effectively a sequel to the Jerry Cornelius novel. I put what I'd written aside and thought about
it all, eventually conceiving the notion of writing a tetralogy
of books about Jerry, each one expanding upon the various
moral questions raised in the *The Final Programme*. I visited
New York in 1967 and told George Ernsberger about my
scheme and George, was, again, enthusiastic. Eventually, in
1968, I had a contract from Avon for the remaining three
books. By this time *The Final Programme* had been bought
by Allison and Busby who were equally enthusiastic and had
also bought *Behold the Man* in its novel version. They, too,
were pleased with the tetralogy idea and guaranteed to publish
them in England. It gave me the necessary encouragement to
carry on with *A Cure For Cancer* which took, in all, some
three years to write, appearing first as a serial in NEW WORLDS.
In 1968 *The Final Programme* was published, at the time
when Jim Sallis had come over to work on NEW WORLDS. Jim
read the book and was very enthusiastic about it. When Lang
Jones was commissioned to edit the big hardback anthology
for Hutchinson, *The New SF*, he asked me for a story and I
decided that I would try to write a Jerry Cornelius story (this
was *The Peking Junction*) – developing some of the techniques
I was beginning to feel happy with while working on *A Cure
For Cancer*. Jim Sallis asked me, then, if I had any objection
to his writing a Jerry Cornelius story since, in his opinion, the
JC stories were a form in themselves. I had none, of course.

He wrote *Jeremiad*, which was published in NEW WORLDS. Taking up part of a theme I'd put into my second JC short, *The Delhi Division*, he expanded from there and wrote an entirely different story. Taking up part of his theme I wrote it back into *Delhi Division*, which he'd so far only seen in rough draft. *The Delhi Division* was the first JC short to appear in NEW WORLDS and was quickly followed by *Jeremiad*. Once this had happened several others who had enjoyed *The Final Programme* felt that they'd like to do a story about Jerry, so shortly afterwards there appeared stories by Brian Aldiss, Norman Spinrad, a poem by Lang Jones, and other stories by M. John Harrison, Maxim Jakubowski and one other by me *The Tank Trapeze*. Most of these were eventually published in a book called *The Nature of the Catastrophe* (Hutchinson, 1971). In the meantime I had also begun a comic strip for IT, then the leading underground paper in Britain, with Mal Dean, who had illustrated many of the JC stories. The IT strip sent up many of the current obsessions of the underground – the mysticism, the political naïvete and so on. We began to alternate, with Mike Harrison and Richard Glyn Jones taking up our themes and us taking up their themes turn by turn. The strip ran for about a year in IT as *The Adventures of Jerry Cornelius, The English Assassin*. Part of the strip was also published in *The Nature of the Catastrophe*. In our terms we found a cool way of dealing with hot material. The essence of the stories is their irony, their attempts to concentrate as much information as possible into as small a space as possible, their obsession with contemporary imagery, their strong reliance on metaphorical imagery drawn from many disparate sources – pop music, astronomy, physics, cybernetics, etc. They are, ideally, deeply serious in intention. Unfortunately many critics have missed the serious points of the stories, even if they've found the stuff entertaining. Sexual ambiguity, for instance, is taken for granted in the JC stories – a fact of life – but critics continue to see that element, among others, as 'daring'. In this country, at any rate, the stories receive their most intelligent responses from that section of the public most at ease with what's these days called the 'alternative' society, was earlier called 'beat' and before that called 'bohemian' – i.e. people who by and large do take certain things for granted which are regarded as shocking by the average middle-class person. I'm not here suggesting that this is good or bad, but it is a fact. Judy Merril, for instance, regarded *The Final Programme* as an 'evil' book. Other people have expressed similar reactions. I find them almost impossible to understand. Perhaps people will get a better idea of the JC novels when the whole tetralogy is complete. *The English Assassin* will be out in England this year, after three years in the writing. I don't know when the last book, *The Condition of Muzak*, will appear – probably in a couple of years, maybe three or four. I'll just have to wait patiently until then. At present, while having reservations about the first two books, I'm very satisfied with *Assassin* – it's the first book of mine I've been able to proof-read without wincing all the way through. Presumably Holt Reinhardt, who did *Cure,* will be doing *Assassin* in the States sometime next year. I haven't had any information either from Avon or from Holt, as yet. Maybe *Final Programme* will get its points across better as a film. The rights have been bought and the script written and its being produced by the company who did *Performance* (which has something in common with *Final Programme*). I heard Jagger turned down the JC part as being too freaky and I don't know if the film ever will be made, but it would be interesting to see how the public reacted to it. I think the JC stories have matured considerably since *Final Programme* – becoming better written and more complex – and it *does* disappoint me when people don't enjoy them or find them obscure. I remember the delight I felt at producing a book which I was sure everyone would find at very least entertaining. I was puzzled when some people reacted in a puzzled or even antagonistic way. My own wavelengths changed somewhere at some time. These days, for instance, I can't understand SF – I read the words and they no longer mean anything to me, even when written by a writer I used to enjoy. So I suppose I can appreciate how people feel when they find a JC story they can't focus on. It isn't, incidentally, anything to do with radical alterations in life-style on my part. It just happened at some point. Ho hum.

(Letter to reader)

IN LIGHTER VEIN

(1976)

A NOTE ON THE JERRY CORNELIUS TETRALOGY

Part of my original intention with the Jerry Cornelius stories was to 'liberate' the narrative; to leave it open to the reader's interpretation as much as possible – to involve the reader in such a way as to bring his own imagination into play. The impulse was probably a result of my interest in Brecht – an interest I'd had since the mid-fifties.

Although the structure of the tetralogy is very strict (some might think over-mechanical) the scope for interpretation is hopefully much wider than of a conventional novel. The underlying logic is also very disciplined, particularly in the last three volumes. It's my view that a work of fiction should contain nothing which does not in some way contribute to the overall scheme. The whimsicalities to be found in all the books are, in fact, not random, not mere conceits, but make internal references. That is to say, while I strive for the effect of randomness on one level, the effect is achieved by a tightly controlled system of internal reference, puns, ironies, logic-jumps which no single reader may fairly be expected to follow.

Thus, in a scene in *Condition of Muzak* (the end of the section called 'Outcast of the Islands'), there is a short discussion about the Japanese invasion of Australia and Jerry makes a reference to big egoes and Hitler. Shakey Mo then asks if he was a character in a children's comic and then immediately asks if Hitler wasn't a police chief they'd met in Berlin. The first reference is to Big Ego (a cartoon ostrich in THE DANDY or THE BEANO); the second reference is to an earlier story of mine (a 'key' story, in my view) called *The Pleasure Garden of Felippe Sagittarius* (where Hitler was a rather pathetic police chief in an imaginary Berlin), leading to a reference to the fact that the historical Adolf Hitler doesn't exist in this world.

All this happens in a couple of sentences or so and should give the effect, among others, of time in a state of flux, men in a state of introverted confusion, close to fugue, and so on. But its internal logic is straightforward : the two characters know exactly what they are talking about. To 'explain' all this, to editoralise, would be to break the mood, break the dramatic tensions, and ruin the effect I was trying to achieve. The apparent obscurity should not confuse the reader because the narrative should be moving so rapidly that he shouldn't care if he doesn't understand every reference. Similarly, if he was watching a richly textured film, he would not expect to perceive consciously every detail of every scene, dialogue, music, etc. The dynamics of the narratives are rarely visible, but they are there. They are maintained primarily by a complicated series of prefiguring images which are developed as the book progresses.

(Note to bibliography)

SAVOY BOOKS

Also available, a unique series of pictorial adaptations of Moorcock fantastry by leading genre artist James Cawthorn

STORMBRINGER

Adapted by James Cawthorn, this very large format illustrated book version of one of Michael Moorcock's famous fantasy novels is an exciting addition to the Moorcock *œuvre* and a must for all collectors of Moorcockiana. Brilliantly drawn in powerful black and white frames, *Stormbringer* tells of 'the time of the heroes' when Elric, last emperor of Melniboné, Lord of Dragons, battled with the hordes of chaos, summoning the Lords of Law to fight for Earth.

£1·00

JEWEL IN THE SKULL

Second in the series of Michael Moorcock illustrated books this is the first story in the famous *Dorian Hawkmoon* series. Two years in the making, this book contains Cawthorn's finest artwork, including many double page splash panels forming an 80 page *tour de force* unparalleled in fantasy graphics. A book destined to be a classic.

Should you have difficulty obtaining these or other SAVOY BOOKS send remittance (inc. p & p) to:

SAVOY BOOKS
3 Whittle Street
Tib Street
Manchester
England